# The Name Field

Sean Boling

Published by Sean Boling, 2018.

This is a work of fiction. Similarities to real people, places, or events are entirely coincidental.

THE NAME FIELD

**First edition. January 8, 2018.**



ISBN: 979-8224355044

Written by Sean Boling.

# CHAPTER ONE: K-2

After each page of his Individualized Education Plan, I asked his mother if she had any questions.

She had comments instead.

"At least he's friendly. He don't sit in a corner rockin' back and forth, makin' noise."

"His older brothers and sisters are all gonna live at home when they grow up. At least Field has an excuse. They're just lazy."

I didn't mind. I was surprised and delighted that his mother even brought him in for the evaluation. I had already worked ten years as a Learning Disability Specialist by that time, so it's not hindsight to say that I had developed a pretty keen sense of which families would follow through on a recommendation and which ones would ignore it. Working in a small town helped, since I was familiar with a lot of the families anyway, but for the most part my instincts were sharpened thanks to recognizing certain characteristics which extend beyond our valley, and still apply all these years later.

Ignoring a teacher's referral, assuming it was a legitimate suggestion, sometimes involved denial, other times oblivion. Denial was more likely to circulate amid the moneyed families, the owners of the vineyards and the olive groves, and of the businesses that served them. Oblivion was more common amongst those who either strung together many jobs at once, or had no job at all.

I had pegged Kathy Spahn as the oblivious type.

When Field's pre-school teacher had contacted me about her recommendation, that one of the Spahn kids may be coming in for an assessment, the shock came from so many directions that my laughter was merely the first inappropriate response.

"Hold on," I needed to back up. "One of the Spahn spawn is in pre-school?"

"Spahn spawn?"

"Spahn children," I grimaced, disappointed in myself for revealing the slang term we used in referring to Kathy's kids.

The young idealist was kind enough to slip past my slip.

"I opened up my school down the street from them last year. I thought it would be neighborly to let him attend."

"For free?"

"Well, at a discount."

"But it's turned out to be free."

"Yes."

"You are neighborly. And very sweet to recommend Field."

"You don't think she'll bring him in?"

"I've tried to get every one of those kids in here."

"Maybe since I'm their neighbor."

"And you haven't complained about them yet?"

"Maybe being a few doors down is just far enough away."

I laughed and repeated the world "maybe". I thanked her and couldn't resist cracking "I'll be holding my breath" as I hung up the phone.

I may as well have been holding my breath when Kathy called, as I lost my capacity to breathe for a couple of heartbeats.

The results of Field's evaluation were not as outside the norm as his family was. He was well within the range of qualifying for an IEP and Special Education, but not to a degree that made the idea of mainstreaming him at some point implausible.

"We may be able to raise his academic goals as he grows up and matures," I told Ms. Spahn.

"Matures," Ms. Spahn sucked on the word. "He'll grow, I'll give you that. His Dad's a big son of a bitch."

Field's IEP was filled with phrases like "has trouble transitioning from one activity to the next", "fixates on a single task", and "frustrates easily". His goals included, "Field will respond to a request without having to be reminded more than three times."

But such was the case for all of his Special Ed classmates. They all had the request-and-reminder goal in their plans. The number of times they would need to be asked varied, as did the ways they ignored those who were asking.

The range of personalities was most apparent when they all happened to be in the same room together, after starting the morning in their mainstream classrooms and being led to the Special Education room for however long their IEPs required.

Some were quiet, saying nothing, not making any noises. Amongst the quiet ones, some projected warmth, seeming content with the world inside themselves, a slight smile granted to those who tried to gain access, while some offered a chill, as though they were trapped in their silence, determined to get out, but wanted to do it on their own, refusing any hand extended their way.

Some were loud, sharing every thought that came to mind, filling in the blank spaces of their monologues with humming or sound effects. Amongst the loud, some tethered themselves to whomever was nearby, asking questions, sharing their ideas, expecting to be understood regardless of how their words piled up, while others didn't appear to care whether anyone was listening, expressing their thoughts aloud while their meaning remained private.

There was a physical faction, a small subset whose inner life met the outer with constant movement. Field had the most in common with this group. He was difficult to categorize, as he dabbled in each cast without starring in any of them, but while his physical idiosyncrasies were no more pronounced than his talking sprees, they were steady. His teachers often had to encourage him to put down the paper and start writing on it, rather than running it up and down his face to sniff it, or graze his cheeks. And while he was hardly the only child in either his mainstream or Special Ed class to massage his temples with the eraser of his pencil, he reached a level of meditation while doing so that required more than words to pull him back into the present, usually a gentle nudge from a teacher, or slightly harder one from a classmate. He developed a method of his own that he called "shake the page." When he caught himself tuning out, he picked up the paper he was working on and wiggled it. He would proudly alert the teacher he was "shaking the page", and the teacher would congratulate him for checking back in on earth.

The smallest division of children in the IEP company was an emotional handful who had no default setting, only highs and lows. They were either in complete silence or a raging fit.

A hierarchy never established itself within the small band of outsiders to whom Field was assigned, due in part to their dispositions, but also the transient nature of their meetings, as they were shuttled to and from their headquarters at designated times. If a leader could have emerged, Lulu would have been the one.

She stopped crying by the time she was four years old. She had cried a lot up until then. Her struggles were so many that she seemed to realize there wasn't enough time to cry over them. Instead she appeared to age, her posture bent, her eyes pleading, walking like an old lady on hot sand. Her family spoke very little English, made very little money, while being very dedicated to insuring she had whatever she needed to reach her modest goals. Observing her family accomplish so much with such a limited ability to communicate and so few means may have demonstrated to her the value of engaging the world regardless of how challenging the engagement may be. She was the kid in the crew most willing to interact with her colleagues in the Special Ed room, even though her efforts were rarely reciprocated. She was also the most willing to give mainstream interaction a try, even though her attempts at bridge-building led to looks and comments from the so-called normal kids that would make most children her age cry, regardless of what classroom they called home. But she had given up crying.

Except on the third day of Kindergarten.

She was running on the grass field beyond the playground. The turf wasn't much softer than the pavement, having been baked over the summer. But there was a miniature swamp hidden in the grass. A sprinkler head had burst in the heat, water gurgling up through the exposed opening and soaking the area around it. Lulu slid in the tiny marsh, leaving her marked with mud on one whole side, ankle to armpit. She was as surprised to find herself muddy as she was to find herself crying. Once she started, though, she let it rip. She was used to mental obstacles. Now the physical was taunting her. She cried as though running out of places in the world where she could function. Her long stints between cries may have also contributed to the intensity, which even took the yard duty by surprise. No one seemed willing to step in, as she appeared capable of popping into an explosion of tears and vanishing if anyone touched her.

Field wasn't worried. Those who knew they were in Special Education together may have claimed he understood her condition. Those who didn't know may have been surprised to find out he was in the same program, with struggles that rivaled hers, given how much he looked the part of a hero as he brought her a handful of paper towels from the bathroom.

They were coarse, like paper towels in public places tend to be, and wadded up into a ball, but they may as well have been a bouquet of white roses.

Lulu thanked him through her tears. She wasn't yet composed enough to put the paper towels to use, so Field did his best to wipe the mud from her.

Only then did the yard duty intervene.

"Hands to yourself," she reminded him.

They obeyed the rule.

They kept their hands to themselves, as they grew inseparable.

In a more primitive time, Field and Lulu may have been child prodigies, rather than drags on their school district's budget and performance metrics. Their sensitivity to noise would keep the tribe safe, their feel for the rhythms of the earth keep everyone fed, and pleasure at working with their hands for as long as it took to complete a project would keep the tribe sheltered. Field and Lulu would one day become sages, healers, elders, whatever the title may be, depending on where in the world they grew up. But they were born into an era buried under centuries of human invention, a place that gave little more than lip service to the natural order of things. There were no predators just outside the village perimeter, so their acute hearing didn't make them heroes, it only prevented them from learning their multiplication tables. Those rumblings in the ground they could feel weren't stampedes or earthquakes or aquifers, they were trucks and airplanes and hundreds of classmates, which kept them from learning to read at the same pace as the rest. There was never enough time to finish what they were doing. It was on to the next subject. It was on to the other room, two buildings away, the room filled with a shifting handful of fellow children whom people pitied but resented.

They would come and go, depending on the subject they were wrestling with, their grade level, and the plan that the adults in their lives had agreed to.

The kids in their cohort were rarely invited to birthday parties. Neither did their families throw many parties to make up for their kids' exclusion. The parents tended to be self-conscious about their children, reversing the traditional roles of kids being embarrassed by their parents. At any event, the parents would form a tense circle around the kids, watching them in preparation to jump in when their child lost control. Their vigilance had the added benefit of allowing them to avoid eye contact with the other parents and the nervous smiles and sympathetic looks that were well-intentioned, but had the effect of prisoners in the yard asking each other, "What are you in for?"

It was easy for the parents to believe their children didn't mind having their names struck from the guest lists, as absorbed in their own realities as their kids appeared to be.

Field and Lulu were able to break through the velvet rope on occasion and score an invitation from a homeroom classmate. Their chances at convention were likely thanks to parental prodding if the party was large enough, and held at a public space rather than someone's house. Field was extended more invites than Lulu, since he wasn't as loud as her. But a pizza place with an arcade, or a laser tag arena, or a bounce house next to a playground were the kinds of stimuli-rich environments that didn't suit either of their needs very well.

They were happiest attending each other's birthday parties.

They were small affairs, thrown by Lulu's family, even when it was Field's birthday.

"Field's family can't have a party for him," Lulu would tell her family. "Can we please, please, please, please, please, please, please, please have a party for him?"

"That's sweet of you, mija," her mother would say. "But that might hurt his family's feelings."

"They're tough," she would insist. "He says they don't worry about anything."

So they compromised, inviting Field over for a playdate then surprising him with a cake, and singing both Happy Birthday and Feliz Cumpleanos, at Lulu's insistence.

"You get two birthday songs this way," she whispered to Field.

She also whispered to him that his party had to be a secret, that her parents didn't want to offend his parents.

It was an easy secret to keep. The Spahns tended not to ask Field how his day went, nor if he had a good time. When it was Lulu's birthday party, and secrecy wasn't necessary, Ms. Spahn sent Field's older sister to escort him, who didn't mind since it meant free food.

"I figure lunch was probably pretty good," Ms. Spahn said after they arrived back home from Lulu's sixth birthday. "But what about the cake? Was it from one of those Mexican bakeries?"

"No, it was good," Field's sister answered. "Ice cream, too. Not shaved ice or nothin'."

"Damn. Maybe I'll go next year. Brush up my Spanish."

"Just bring your phone," Field's sister shrugged.

"Seriously?" their mother barked. "You just batted around on that thing the whole time?"

"So?"

"I swear, you older kids are more embarrassing than Field sometimes. Where's your manners?"

"At least I went."

Which is a claim she could throw not only at her mother, but most of the other families from the Special Education program who received hand-written invitations from Lulu in their children's folders.

The most likely to show up were the quiet kids, whose parents didn't have to worry about an outburst, aside from some low-volume noises and maybe some sobbing. Field and Lulu liked having those classmates attend, since they could show them how to play the party games and encourage them to swing the plastic bat and hit the piñata, rather than study the bat's color and contours, which was often their preference. Lulu gave each of them two hugs while she opened her gifts, one when she read whom the gift was from, and another after she discovered what it was. She would hug Field an extra-long time until they started to giggle and fall over.

"Hands to yourself," they would be reminded at school when they did the same thing on the playground.

Field always had rocks in his pockets that he collected from the nooks and crannies in the school landscaping. He would present Lulu with the ones that sparkled or appeared to have streaks of silver in them.

When they ate lunch together, neither appeared to notice the other's mealtime quirks. Field would touch every bite of food against two parts of his face, usually his cheeks or eyebrows, one at a time, before eating it. Sometimes he would go with his ears. First the left, then the right, each a light tap so as to avoid leaving any traces of peanut butter or crumbs, though that often happened anyway thanks to the repetition. Lulu didn't have a ritual so much as a position. She liked to perch on her seat rather than sit in it, resembling an ancient presence crouched by a fire ready to fight or take flight should someone or something try to snatch her food.

They attended different mainstream classes when they weren't in Special Ed together. Their teachers thought it best to encourage them to branch out and perhaps make some additional friends, but the kids in their homerooms weren't interested. They weren't mean, at least not often or overtly, but did keep their distance.

Field tried to make some friends online when he earned the right to play games on the classroom computer on Friday afternoons. His family didn't have one at home, so he was proud of himself and excited at the idea of talking to kids from around the whole wide world. But even between children, the online community was ruthless. They played math games with Field, simple scenarios involving basic arithmetic, but he couldn't complete them without help. He didn't ask for that help because this was his time, a chance to feel bigger, and the online opponents typed comments that he didn't understand were sarcastic.

"Great job, dopey."

"Way to suck, smarty."

How could he do a great job if he was a dope? How could he suck if he was smart?

He asked his teacher.

"Just play the games on your own, Field, against the computer. Don't invite anyone to play with you."

Lulu played the math games with him, and he didn't need to ask her. They would get everything wrong together and laugh when the cartoon raccoon would make a surprised face and a speech bubble would pop up saying, "OOPS. Almost. Try again!"

They would read it aloud. They were always proud when they could read something. They needed help with the word "again" when they first saw it, but the words quickly became theirs, and not only during Friday afternoon math games.

They used the words every time they whiffed while trying to slap the tether ball as it swung past.

"OOPS. Almost. Try again!"

They would imitate the raccoon's surprised face and send each other into hysterics.

Every time the hula hoop spun down their legs to the ground. Every time they tried to throw the volleyball into the basketball hoop. Every time they mispronounced a word on a flashcard, even if they were in different groups on opposite ends of the Special Ed room, one would call out to the other.

"OOPS. Almost. Try again!"

And they would both make the face.

They usually were in different groups on opposite ends of the room.

"Hands to yourself" morphed into "Safe hands" as they moved up from one grade to the next. The principal liked the idea of including the word "safe". To the kids, it provided a reason for why hands should be kept to one's self. To the adults, it provided legal cover. To Field and Lulu, it provided more evidence that nothing could keep them apart.

"We're getting married someday," Field told his Mom.

"We love each other like you guys do," Lulu told her parents.

"But we met later in life, mija," they told her.

"You need to marry someone smarter than you," Field's mother told him.

They didn't actually pass each grade, but were moved along on speculation, the idea that they would eventually catch up as their work in Special Education led to some breakthroughs. They managed to reach most of the benchmarks on their IEPs. They increased the number of words they could read in a certain amount of time, decreased the amount of time needed to put random digits in their place along a number line, and responded more promptly to requests. Progress in those areas was incremental, so much the product of hard work and gradual recognition that none could truly be labeled a breakthrough. Sudden leaps were social rather than academic, occurring in the company of other children, as everyone started to grow more aware of the divergent routes into which each group was mapped.

A pair of boys in his second grade homeroom were talking about girls one morning, and Field told them he had a girlfriend, too.

"That ugly girl?" one of them said.

He spent his weekends and school holidays at home for the most part, in his room, or in the backyard. He wasn't trusted to go on playdates, his family couldn't afford to go anywhere, and his siblings stayed away at their jobs, other people's houses, the park, and the shopping center. He would get excited when he'd see one of them hanging around with their friends outside the grocery store when he and his Mom would run errands on the first of the month. He'd wave and shout their name. His sibling would wince and make the pack of friends laugh by rolling out some version of the same joke all the Spahn kids used against each other, that they were only half-brothers and half-sisters. The best was a play on "My Dad can beat up your Dad." The worst was "My Dad is smarter than your Dad," because it was directed exclusively at Field, though never to his face.

He thought a lot about what those boys said, that Lulu was ugly, during the long days talking to himself in the backyard. Sometimes he shared his thoughts with their dog, who paced inside a chain-linked holding area as though on display at an outdated zoo. Other times he would lie down on his back in the weeds. They rose above him on all sides, the sky peeking out from the opening created by his body.

Sometimes he fantasized about punching the boys, really graceful punches and spin kicks like in the video games his brothers played on their phones, and the boys at school would simply stand there in shock and let Field whale away on them. Then he would think about that Special Ed classmate who would have a fit and attack someone who said something he didn't like. It was nothing like the video games. It was sloppy and nerve-wracking, and everyone watching would either stare in disbelief or cry as his classmate had to be restrained by the para-educator assigned to follow him around, and at least one other yard duty. His classmate sounded like the stray cat his sister's Dad once trapped in a cage, making noises somewhere between a grunt and a scream. The classmate would disappear for days afterwards, and eventually he vanished altogether, transferring to another school.

So Field wondered what it would be like to cut the boys down with his words, which was even more unrealistic. He couldn't come up with anything clever enough or cruel enough as he stared at the sky or at the ceiling in his room.

He shared the room with one of his brothers who usually spent the night at his girlfriend's house, so Field considered himself lucky to be able to use the CD player on the nightstand between their beds. He didn't like his brother's music, which was loud and agitating, and he only had one CD of his own, but it was all he needed. The CD was called *Symphony of the Ocean*. It was mostly recordings of whales calling to one another, with some gulls chirping in occasionally, and soft synthesizer music playing in the background. He won it on a field trip to the aquarium when he correctly answered a question about how mother otters carry their babies.

"On their chest," he said.

"Close to their heart," Lulu added.

She won a tiny otter bean bag for her contribution.

The CD was relaxing. Whether he needed to fall asleep, or think about something longer than he was capable of without the whales' help, their songs were a reliable comfort. But even their music did not guide him to a place where he could imagine insulting the boys beyond response. There was no fantasy version he could construct that would not collapse upon entering reality.

He thought about a lesson he learned from an episode of Thomas the Tank Engine on a DVD he used to watch before it accumulated too many scratches and smudges to work anymore. Everyone was laughing at Henry, the big green engine, after he was splashed with water by a circus elephant, and they finally stopped when he laughed along with them. But they weren't laughing at something mean. The elephant splashed him by accident.

Field wasn't even sure the boys were trying to be mean. Neither of them laughed when they said Lulu was ugly. His class had learned about fact and opinion, and Field was convinced their statement was an opinion. He thought about all the other girls in his class and his homeroom, and any others he had encountered on the playground or in the multipurpose room on rainy days. Why would anyone consider Lulu ugly compared to them? Was it her eyes? They stuck out, but Field liked that. She always seemed excited by whatever she was doing or wherever she was. She was really skinny, but that was common. She had thick hair, which people complimented her on. There didn't seem to be much difference between her and the other girls. Whatever it was that made people think she was ugly, it was a matter of an inch here and there, maybe less than an inch. If her eyes were even a tiny bit less bulgy, or if she stood up a bit more straight, those boys would never have said anything. They may not have thought she was pretty, but at least they would not have an opinion.

They were butt noses.

Adding "butt" or "nose" to anything always made him laugh, so he used both words at the same time in his mind whenever he saw those boys.

He told Lulu about his nickname for them. She asked why he called them that, and he told her what they said about her.

He thought she would be grateful. He was standing up for her. Kind of.

"Kind of" were her words.

She said them after a long silence that confused Field. She looked sad, but the kind of sad she showed when she realized her finger had dipped a bit and she was dragging it along the line with multiples of six, rather than seven, and would have to do the problem over.

"I'm going to call them butt noses right to their faces," he tried harder to impress her.

"You don't need to tell me that, Field."

"I should just do it," he agreed.

"No," she pleaded. "I mean you don't need to tell me what they said."

"Oh."

"Don't ever tell me any mean things people say. Not ever."

"Okay."

"Promise."

"I promise."

She looked down and seemed to sniff the flowers printed on her shirt.

Field had no trouble keeping his promise to Lulu. The boys never said anything else to him. Neither did any of the other kids.

They were developing manners.

They would look and whisper to each other instead. And Lulu could see that.

# CHAPTER TWO: 3-5

Lulu loved that flower shirt.

And her puppy shirt.

She loved her shirt with the smiling strawberries on it. Their eyes were so wide open. Of all her shirts with smiling faces on it, the strawberries were her favorite.

Field loved his zoo shirt.

His great aunt took him to the zoo once when she was in town. It was a long drive, so his siblings didn't go. When they returned home, he was going to tell his siblings how wrong they were, how worth it the drive was. So when his aunt offered to buy him a souvenir, he chose a shirt that had a drawing of a bunch of animals in a car. Underneath the car it said, "Going To The Zoo!", and the animals all looked so excited. There was a tiger, a lion, a bear, an elephant, a giraffe, and a bird on the giraffe's head. They were all smiling. Field wore it at least once a week, sometimes more.

He wanted to get a bigger one as he started to outgrow it, but nobody wanted to drive to the zoo, and his great aunt had died. He asked one of his teachers to help him look on the zoo's website to see if he could buy one online, but they couldn't find the same shirt.

"They must have discontinued that design," his teacher told him.

Which was somewhat the case for all the shirts Field and Lulu loved to wear.

Even if their favorite designs were still available, they weren't available in the larger sizes they were growing into. So they wore them as long as they could, until pulling them over their heads squeezed their ears, and the sleeves pinched their armpits.

Once the shirt was finally on, Field liked the snug fit, the feeling of someone hugging him tightly.

T-shirts were the only thing Field's mother ever offered to buy him during their monthly shopping day.

"They don't have shirts I like," he said as he slouched through the selections in the Boys Department.

"Then get some plain ones."

"Those are boring."

"Then grow up and get over the little kid stuff. Be a big boy already."

He drifted back to the toddler shelves while she wasn't looking and tried desperately to get a Peppa Pig shirt on, but couldn't even get it down his arms to his head.

"You're gonna rip it!" his mother hissed, struggling to pull it off from behind him. "And even if it did fit, you'd look like an idiot. I don't even think it's for a boy, much less one your age."

She wadded it up and shoved it onto the shelf next to her.

"That's not where it goes," Field said.

"Who gives a shit," she bayed. "Just get back to where you're supposed to be and pick out some goddamn shirts."

"You're swearing a lot."

"They'll have to call security on me in a minute if you don't get over there."

"Okay, okay," Field moped.

"This ain't just about you drivin' me crazy," she stalked him back to the Boys Department. "You can't go around lookin' like we ain't bought you clothes in, like, forever. If only your brothers hadn't sold their old clothes..."

They arrived back where they started and she gestured to the shirts.

"Go nuts," she said. "You need at least five. Let me handle the pants. I need a break anyway. Don't go nowhere till I get back."

At least he still had his bedsheets.

They had trains on them, all different kinds, and looked like they had been drawn by other little kids. He wished he could have some of his drawings printed on bedsheets that other kids would see.

He saw the same kind of pattern on some kitchen towels he passed while barely keeping up with his mother as she whisked around the store. Instead of trains, however, the kitchen towels had farm animals on them

"I wonder if real little kids drew them, or if it was grown-ups drawing like little kids," he wondered out loud next to a woman who was surveying the kitchen wares with a slight smile on her face, determined to pretend he wasn't there.

"What do you think?" he asked her.

"About what, dear?" she asked back.

"Do you think real kids drew these animals?" he grabbed a dish towel hanging from a rack and held it up.

"I...maybe."

"I have a feeling it's grown-ups pretending."

"Oh. I could see that."

"They did a good job if it is."

"The certainly did."

"Are you gonna buy any of it?"

"I don't have a farm animal theme in my kitchen."

"What's a theme?"

"Well, it's...uh..."

"Let's go, Field," his mother cut in and swiped the towel from his hand. She crammed it back onto the rack while apologizing to the woman.

"It's okay," the woman smiled.

Field kissed the woman's forearm.

"Oh, for God's sake," his mother groaned as she latched onto his forearm.

The woman was caught between reactions.

"You're way too old to still be doin' that," his mother muttered as she led him away.

"Bye," Field looked back at the woman.

"Bye," she said, mustering a wave in the midst of her confusion.

The phrase "safe hands" started to lose ground to "don't interrupt."

It was a close race.

Sometimes Lulu said it to him. Their teacher would be explaining why "gh" sometimes makes the "f" sound, and Field would start wondering out loud what all the other words with Fs in them would look like if they were spelled with GH.

"Shhh," Lulu said. "Don't interrupt."

Sometimes what he interrupted with had nothing to do with what was being said around him. His sister would talk on her phone to a friend, the conversation revolving around some other girl they thought was a back stabber, a fake, a game-player, and Field would tell her that there was a sunken Pizza Planet truck in *Finding Dory*.

"What?" his sister lowered her phone and scrunched up her face.

"We watched *Finding Dory* in class. We earned it. They swim by a Pizza Planet delivery truck in one scene. It's underwater."

"So?"

"Pizza Planet is from Toy Story. It's an Easter Egg."

His sister didn't say "Don't interrupt." She sighed and raised the phone back up to her ear, turned away, and picked up on the picking on.

Field often performed dialogue between himself and Lulu when she wasn't around. He would pace, walk in circles, and quietly improvise a conversation, playing both parts, no matter where he happened to be when the urge struck.

When he was in a large group of people, it was certain to happen, much to the consternation of whoever was with him, usually his mother. When it happened at a school assembly one day while he tried to sit with his homeroom class waiting for the presentation to start, a classmate heard him say Lulu's name as part of his one-man show before it was cut short by his teacher asking him to sit down and hush.

"Do you pretend you're talking to me?" Lulu asked him later in Special Ed.

"Who told you?"

"Don't worry. I'm happy about it."

She hugged him quickly to avoid any cries of "Safe hands," but he was still embarrassed.

"Do you imagine we're on an adventure?" she asked.

He nodded.

"Where do we go?"

"We play sports."

Lulu was surprised. She expected time travel and dinosaurs.

Field explained.

"When the kids in homeroom get out early on Friday afternoons to go play basketball at another school, we go with them."

"Boys and girls play on different teams."

"It doesn't matter because you're the best."

"I am?"

"You play on the boys team, and I pass you the ball all the time."

"And I shoot it!"

"And you score!"

"All the time!"

"Because you're the best!"

Lulu giggled and Field shared another play he often wrote.

"We play in the band, too."

"Really?"

"When the kids in homeroom leave class and pick up their instruments, we go with them."

"What do we play?"

"I play the drums, and you play the tuba."

"The tuba? They don't even have a tuba in the band room."

"It doesn't matter, because your name sounds like it came out of a tuba. Loo, loo, loo, loo, loo..."

She laughed and joined him in repeating the sound of her name in the lowest voices they could reach.

They finally did get a chance to perform for the school as their time inside of it was winding down. The fifth grade class performed a dance to celebrate their transition into middle school. There were also awards ceremonies. Field received a Most Improved certificate, and Lulu was granted one for being a Good Citizen, but all they had to do for those assemblies was walk up and accept their pieces of paper. The dance was one of Field's dreams made real, an opportunity to live one of the fantasies he had crafted and shared with his best friend.

They rehearsed relentlessly. Every time they met in the playground, they practiced the steps, whispering the lyrics to the song as their own accompaniment. They had never heard of Tina Turner before, nor her song "Simply the Best", but they liked how the song allowed them to say things like "you're simply the best" to each other while they practiced, and "better than all the rest."

Each rehearsed on their own at home, and they held each other accountable during their playground sessions. If they got frustrated with one another, the lyrics to the song would help. "Better than anyone, anyone I ever met."

They laughed at the lyrics that had to do with fire and passion.

"This isn't for kids," Field said at the same time he was laughing.

"Didn't they listen to all the words?" Lulu asked nobody in particular, but Field answered anyway.

"I guess not."

Lulu went with it.

"They just heard 'Simply the Best' and were all, 'yeah, perfect.'"

"I still like it."

"Let's just practice some more, Field."

"Okay, Lulu."

Their hard work led to something as close to perfection as they had ever come. They knew the steps better than anyone. If it had been a test, they would have been at the top of the class, the fifth grade class, not just their Special Ed class.

As they performed the final turn, which involved a big step forward, a pivot, a big step back, and a spin to face the audience again, their stern expressions of concentration broke into smiles when all that was left for each to do was thrust their right arm into the air, fist clenched. They smiled at the cheering crowd of parents and children from the lower grades, then smiled at each other.

They held the pose longer than anyone else, not wanting the moment to end.

Their classmates peeled away, rushing off stage in both directions toward their awaiting families and friends.

Field and Lulu slowly lowered their arms until they were simply standing side-by-side. Their smiles had faded, replaced by deep breaths of satisfaction, inhaling as many details as they could to build the most accurate possible memory, while each exhale started to push it into the past.

When they ran out of building materials, and their breathing and their lives returned to normal, they hugged each other tightly and no one said "safe hands" or "hands to yourself". They nearly fell over in their clutch, as they did in Kindergarten the first time they hugged.

"You were perfect," Lulu giggled.

"So were you," Field giggled back.

They smiled at one another a few more seconds before Lulu's mother called to her. They both turned to see her whole family waving.

Lulu waved back, then started to run before she caught herself and reached back for Field.

"Come on!"

They ran hand-in-hand off stage, down the stairs, and were greeted by hugs from each family member, not just her Mom and Dad, but her siblings too.

"You were so good!" her Mom said to both of them. "Like professionals."

Their smiles said "I know" on their behalf.

"Field!" his mother yelled.

Field's eyes bulged at the sound of her voice, and jaw dropped upon spying her approach.

"You came!" he ran into her arms.

"Good stuff, baby!" she welcomed his embrace.

He noticed his sister as he emerged from their hug.

"Nice job, Field," his sister smiled a bit.

"You guys are proud of me," he observed.

"We sure are," his Mom said.

"Hey, Lulu," he beamed her way. "Look, my Mom's here."

Lulu spun around to address her parents.

"Can they come over?" she asked in Spanish.

"We're having a party," she explained in English to Field and his Mom and sister.

"Oh, that's okay, honey," Field's Mom said. "You have your party. Don't you worry. We're takin' Field out to celebrate."

"Really?" Field cried.

"Slurpees sound good?"

"Yes!" he cried even louder.

"Bye, Lulu," he turned to give her a goodnight hug. "See you next week."

"Next week is going to be so easy," Lulu said as they untangled themselves.

"Games and cleanup," Field remembered.

"And treats," Lulu added.

"From two different classrooms," Field further added.

"And no homework!" Lulu topped off the list.

"We're so lucky!" Field said as each of their families guided them away with exasperated chuckles.

With their families in tow, Field and Lulu essentially floated toward the doors on opposite ends of the multi-purpose room. They passed their classmates and their families, and noticed them complimenting each other. Field was excited enough by the compliments he received from his Mom and sister that he wasn't looking for any others. But Lulu thought they had earned some praise from the outside, from someone, anyone, other than their families.

There were some grins aimed their way, but no compliments.

She was unusually quiet over the weekend.

Her Mom noticed as Lulu ate the lunch she had prepared for her on Saturday, and asked her if she was okay.

"Nobody noticed me and Field were the best," she answered.

"That's okay, mija. We know you did a good job, and you know."

"We did the best job."

"And you should be proud."

Lulu was proud.

But she was not satisfied.

She compared her experience with Field as they cleaned out their desks, asked if anyone else had congratulated him besides his family.

"No," he didn't see a problem.

Lulu stopped pulling things from her desk and placing them into the garbage bag between them and instead started jerking and slamming them.

"What's wrong?" Field asked.

"We finally did it," she was near tears. "We beat them. And nobody cares."

Field took a break from emptying his desk and retraced what he recalled about the assembly.

"They did fine," he concluded.

"We were better," she insisted. "We worked harder. We always work harder. But this time it wasn't just to keep up. We won."

When I sat down with them individually to help plan their schedules for middle school, they each brought up the assembly, Field out of confusion, and Lulu out of determination.

"It isn't fair," Lulu said.

She had grown up so much, but still didn't fill out the chair that sat across from me.

"You've always been so wise when it comes to fairness," I told her. "You understood life wasn't fair earlier than anyone I've ever met."

"I'm only talking about one time," she responded. "Not life. Just one time that's fair. Everyone gets those."

She paused. Her petulance vanished.

"Don't they?" she asked.

Her voice was so soft. I couldn't remember her saying anything so quietly. Measuring my reply took more effort than usual.

I was good at not making promises I couldn't keep to the students in my case files. The challenge was wording a cautious message that didn't sound discouraging.

"Everyone gets at least one," I decided to say.

"When will mine be?"

"I can't answer that. But I think it's safe to hope for more than one."

During Field's appointment, he was more interested in the compliments themselves, rather than whether they represented some sort of victory.

"Did you notice how good we were?" he asked me.

"I certainly did. You were great."

"You've said that to us before. Lots of times."

"I always mean it."

"It would be nice to have someone new say something."

"People are focused on their own kids, Field. They don't pay attention to any of the others, not matter how good or bad they are."

"Even my Mom paid attention that night," he agreed with me. "And my sister."

"How could they not?"

"Is that why people do things?"

"What do you mean?" I asked.

"So other people will tell them how good they are?"

"Maybe some people. But doing things just to get rewarded shouldn't always be the reason."

Field stopped talking and started thinking, perhaps about what I said.

"How did you feel up there that night?" I wanted to know.

"Excellent," he smiled.

"That was a pretty good reason to do it, then, right?"

"Right."

We set about designing his middle school schedule, when he would meet for small group sessions, who would be running those meetings, and how often he would be trusted to move from class to class without an escort.

He liked that idea.

"I'll be like everyone else," he mused. "Nobody will know where I'm going."

Though he was concerned about how that would affect his time with Lulu.

"You'll always have the playground," I said, then caught myself. "Well, there's no playground at middle school. But you'll have recess and lunch."

"There's no playground?"

"No."

"What do people do at recess and lunch?"

"They talk. And eat."

"Like grown-ups."

"Yes," I smiled.

He smiled too.

"Me and Lulu," he pondered. "Grown-ups."

We laughed about that together.

I felt like stopping before he did, but kept going for his sake.

# CHAPTER THREE: MIDDLE SCHOOL

Field was considered on time if he arrived within three minutes after the start of each class. That was the agreement. He needed to wait out the horde of bodies that swarmed the halls between periods, and the voices, screams, and laughs that accompanied them.

He would stay behind in the room where class ended and wait for the vibrations in the corridor to subside. He sat by the teacher's desk so it looked to the students who entered for the next class that he was receiving additional help, which was true often enough. He felt fortunate. Not only for the chance to walk the emptied halls, but for the minutes before when he was able to straddle two classes, the one he was in and the one after. He was doubling his contacts. There was a fresh batch of students in middle school who didn't attend his elementary school, who didn't know him as one of those kids ferrying between homeroom and Special Ed, and in his space between the periods, he could see them. Instead of a kaleidoscope of eyes, noses, mouths, hair, ears, and the ambient smells and noises, he was able to focus on each person.

The way he was able to zoom in on them seemed to translate to his school work. He was finally catching up, to a point where he was receiving grades. Not good ones, but grades nonetheless.

Lulu was the other way around. She dealt with the shuffling throng of the shift changes well enough, but the academics continued to elude her.

They had one group study period together, which was right before lunch, so for most of sixth grade they were allowed to stay in the room during break and eat in one other's company. Field no longer touched each bite of food to each side of his face. He was hungrier and ate more than he used to, and the ritual would have slowed him down. Lulu no longer perched on her chair. She was too big and it was too hard to balance. The only remnant of their past idiosyncrasies was a propensity to fidget, which of course is not a rare quality in adolescence, but they were a bit more fidgety than average.

They talked about their classes, their teachers, things they saw on their way to school or on their way home. Lulu's family subscribed to a streaming video service, so she kept Field up to date on the latest anime series she was watching. She described the characters, the world they lived in, and told him the story as it unfolded.

Story time was the closest they came to recapturing their elementary school days. They no longer spoke of marriage. They were old enough for those kinds of words to mean something.

They were more competitive. As much as Field enjoyed Lulu telling him about the latest series she was binging, he started to feel he needed to contribute more to their conversation. He simply didn't have much material until spring came around.

His PE teacher, looking for ways to fill the waning days of the school year, invited the assistant wrestling coach from the high school to demonstrate some basic holds.

"And he chose me to help!" Field told Lulu.

"I know why," she smirked.

"Because I'm the biggest kid in the class."

"Yup," she giggled.

"He needed someone big so it wouldn't look weird when he showed us the moves."

After a week's worth of demonstrations, Field became familiar with the basics, enough so that the following week he was able to work the room with the coach, wandering through the pairs of students practicing the maneuvers and giving them tips on how to do them better.

"You really took to this," the coach smiled at him and put a hand on his shoulder as the wrestling section ended. "Like a fish to water."

Field chuckled.

"You never heard that expression before?"

"I'm not laughing at that," he explained. "I don't take to many things. Not fast."

The coach looked him over.

"Want to learn more?"

Field bobbed his head.

"Over the summer the team works out to get ready for the fall season. Care to join us?"

"On the team?"

"Not yet," the coach laughed. "You have to make it to high school first. But we'll get you ready."

"Thanks, Coach Gonzalez."

"The guys on the team call me Gonzo."

Field told Lulu over lunch and she nearly fell out of her chair.

"Gonzo?" she repeated through her cackling.

"He said if he was head coach then he probably wouldn't let people call him that. But he says he's there to help guys remember to have a good time."

"I'm so happy for you, Field," Lulu came over and hugged him. "It's like the dance we did. You're gonna be the best at something."

Being the best would have to wait, but trying to get there felt good.

The boys on the team welcomed him and treated him like one of their own. The only teenagers he had known up until then were his half-siblings, so it was the first time a group of teenagers had been nice to him.

"I'm glad you're not old enough to try out," said Yadier, a senior who was captain of the team. "You'd take my spot."

Field blushed and didn't know what to say.

Yadier slapped him on the arm and hollered at one of the freshmen, "I guess he'll be taking yours."

The freshman laughed.

A bunch of the other boys looked at each other and grinned, which made the freshman nervous.

"He'll be junior varsity when I'm varsity," he said.

"Just keep telling yourself that," Yadier snickered.

Coach Gonzo would give him a ride to and from practice. On the way home, they would stop by Gonzo's favorite taqueria, the oldest one in town that looked like they occasionally needed to pull up some floor boards and throw them under the grill to keep the fire going. While Field ate, Gonzo would drill him on what he learned that day.

Field had grown too big to have his appetite satisfied by the boxes of wrapped food stacked in the garage that were sometimes empty by the third week of the month, depending on how often his siblings ate at home. So he never refused an invitation to eat with the coach, no matter how guilty he felt about not being able to pay him back.

"You can pay me back by becoming state champion," Coach would say.

Field would smile.

It sounded good, but didn't seem possible.

The head coach never made such a bold prediction.

"He doesn't compliment anyone," Gonzo explained. "He wants to keep everyone hungry. If a kid works hard enough all four years, he'll praise him at the awards banquet senior year. Then and only then."

"I want to get that compliment," Field decided. "Even if I don't win a championship."

"You're a good kid."

Gonzo raised his paper cup with the straw sticking out of the lid as a toast to that goodness.

Nobody else imagined anything so lofty in Field's future.

Certainly not his family. They did appreciate Coach Gonzo giving Field a lift and giving him something to do, almost as much as the gifts he would bring them.

Gonzo was a manager at the enormous home improvement store in the shopping center on the edge of town that had expanded the city limits. Part of picking up and dropping off Field involved Gonzo assessing the withered Spahn residence and delivering some of what it needed next time or on his off days. He would even bring an employee along with the item if specialized labor was needed to install it, such as a window. Other times he would do it himself, if it was a quick job like a new door knob or spraying some weed killer along the front path.

The effort Gonzo made on their behalf provided a clue as to Field's potential, but his family hardly acknowledged his talent. They may have preferred not to imagine one of their own rising above them. They may have decided ignorance looked better than jealousy.

Even Lulu was reluctant to acknowledge what was happening to Field. She accused him of bragging, and searched for a talent of her own.

She tried to revisit the experience of practicing the fifth grade dance with Field, but it wasn't the same without him. And when she saw the middle school dance team perform at an assembly, they moved like girls who had been taking dance since they were toddlers, around the age she was first diagnosed with learning problems and her spare time was cornered by tutoring rather than dance, sports, or art.

Sports also seemed to have already gone through a sorting process and fixed on the most worthy. Likewise music.

Art appeared to have an opening. It offered a chance to think about what she was doing while she was doing it without missing a step, a shot, or a note.

She wanted to draw pictures of her Special Ed classmates. She wanted to draw them so well that they would be displayed someplace prominent on campus, or perhaps at one of the nice hotels that catered to the wine tourists. She knew reaching that level would require a lot of practice, but "a lot" became more defined with each failed attempt, and the definition was frustrating.

Drawing classmates from memory made her task more challenging, but she didn't want to ask anyone to pose for her until she improved enough so as not to be embarrassed when they inevitably asked to see what she had drawn. This forced her into months' worth of self-portraits. If she could draw her own nose, she could draw any nose, her thinking went.

Noses were not the problem. Nor were lips, or even hair. She liked layering all the lines to build a head of hair.

Eyes were. Bringing life to a pair of eyes flummoxed her, to a point where her Mom suggested she try drawing nature.

"Like the oak trees or the vineyards," she said. "Or the hills."

"Everyone does that around here. I want to draw people."

"Maybe you should start with cartoon characters."

"I want to draw people who don't get drawn."

Field was the first person she was willing to ask to model for her, toward the end of seventh grade. Their schedules were due to change substantially the following year, and they would not have as much time together. His mainstream course load was being increased, and they were not going to be in the same tutoring session before lunch, sharing those moments in their shelter as the world churned outside.

She was confident enough that when the bell rang and Field asked to see what she had done, she turned the pad toward him with a flourish.

"It's great!" he gushed.

"Really?"

"Yes!" he confirmed. "You're getting so good!"

It was the best parts of elementary school all over again. She spun the drawing back around to admire it. Instead of basking in the compliment, though, the spin toppled her.

"What?" Field asked as he saw her face slacken.

"The eyes," she lamented.

"What about them?"

"They're mine, not yours."

"They look good," Field assured her.

He turned his attention to his lunch, leftovers from Gonzo's favorite tacqueria. The coach brought the food to the house the night before, along with a new eighteen-inch stand fan to replace the one broken by his older brothers, who rolled into it during a fight.

"They're not right," Lulu held her ground and glared at him as he took a bite of his half burrito.

He looked back at her and replied by slowing down his chewing.

"It looks good," she persisted. "But it's wrong."

Field swallowed his bite.

"Do you want to draw me again?"

"You're not even on the team," she said.

"What?"

"You're like one of those guys who dresses up in a costume and gets the crowd cheering."

"A mascot?"

"Yes. They bring you to the games and let you stand there with the team so they can rub your head and give you high fives."

"They're not called games. They're called meets."

"They're using you."

"I like it."

"They get to think they're helping a special needs kid, but they get something out of it."

She was near tears.

Field wanted to see if they would fall.

Lulu managed to keep them in.

"I'm sorry your drawing didn't turn out," he said.

He packed up his lunch and went outside.

Lulu imagined him at the picnic tables by the gym, with the kids who were pouncing at the opportunity to be around him now.

For the first time since the third day of Kindergarten, when she slipped in the mud and Field came to her rescue with a glob of paper towels, she cried.

By eighth grade it was as if they never knew each other.

Lulu's parents approached Field at the promotion ceremony on the last day of middle school to congratulate him on how far he had come. They were one of many who lined up to wish him their best, who wanted to say they "knew him when", before he became the athletic star he was anointed to be by the local news and accompanying gossip.

Lulu held back, trailing behind her family, prepared to say "I told you so" when he barely gave them a smile and any more time than he did to the sycophants nuzzling up to him.

But he was delighted to see them. Maybe he had grown used to seeing Lulu around, making it easier to forget how much they had meant to each other, and the sight of her family was a jolt to his conscience. Field hugged Lulu's mother as tightly as if she was an opposing wrestler, albeit one who only came up to his shoulders.

"So big now," she beamed at him.

"Especially his head," Lulu muttered.

Her father back-handed her on the arm.

"It's true," she defended herself.

"What's going on?" Field grinned at them, unaware of the exchange.

"Congratulations, Field," her father extended his hand and pretended nothing was going on.

Field shook it and thanked him.

That left Field and Lulu.

It left them for several long seconds.

"Well," Field struck first. "We made it."

"We did," Lulu nodded. "To high school."

"See you there," he said.

"See you," she said.

They shook hands, as though settling on a contract. The terms of agreement appeared to involve no admission of past association, as they mutated into different people and camped with others who fit their new descriptions.

Such a move was common, of course, but Field and Lulu were not common. It broke my heart to see them reach that same old treaty.

They expressed no malice toward the other during my meetings with each of them. Their drift was a part of life, they consoled me, nothing more. They were right, but their assurances were not as comforting as they intended.

A traceable rift, a glaring conflict would provide a source to address, a wall to climb. But there was little use fighting the natural order of things.

# CHAPTER FOUR: HIGH SCHOOL

The man started to appear at the final matches of his freshman year.

Field noticed his Mom cozying up to him. They would stand to the side of the bleachers near the exit and they would flirt with each other like the high school kids sitting above them.

She always preferred that Field catch a ride with Coach Gonzo after the meets because she didn't want to wait around, but on those nights when the strange man started to show up, Field arrived home well before her, and would hear her trying to be quiet as she staggered in much later.

One night he waited up for her like a parent, and when she tried to sneak in, he asked her who that man was.

"Your father," she said, as though he should have known.

"I never saw him before," he responded to her tone.

"You did when you were real little," she seemed to realize his confusion was legitimate.

"Why doesn't he hang out with us after the meet?"

She shrugged.

"I invite him."

"You do?" Field snapped.

"You just asked why he don't hang out with us."

Field couldn't figure out a way to express the problem.

"Well..." he surrendered. "Stop doing that."

"He's proud of you. He's been seein' your name in the news."

"There's no money in wrestling."

"What do you mean?"

"The coach makes that clear. Not like if someone is great at baseball or basketball. We do it because we love it."

"Okay."

"Let him know that."

"He probably knows already. He played sports in high school, too."

Field paused, as though reloading.

"I don't want him to come to the meets anymore."

"He can come if he wants to."

"I'll bet if I told Gonzo, he'd make him stop."

"Don't tell Gonzo."

"Why? You think he wants you back?"

"No."

"Or maybe you don't want Gonzo to know you're creeping around with Dad so you can hit on Gonzo."

His mother glared at him.

"My sweet little boy," she pursed her lips. "You're just like the rest of 'em now."

She went to her room and left Field alone to fret over what he said.

He tapped on the door to no reply.

He apologized the next morning to no eye contact.

Eventually she spoke to him about everyday items, and he stopped trying to bring up anything beyond.

The season ended and all the team did was train, so there was more free time after school. Gonzo taught him how to drive. In the empty parking lot behind the high school on a Sunday, Field told him about his father and how his mother was handling the reappearance.

"The past is thicker than blood," Gonzo told him.

Field wasn't sure what he meant. Gonzo explained that it doesn't matter who someone is, it matters what they do.

They climbed out of the car to switch places, and before ducking back into their seats, Gonzo tapped on the roof to get Field's attention.

"You owe him nothing," he said.

Field found those words to be just as helpful, but they wouldn't look as good on a picture frame or inside a fortune cookie, so he adopted "the past is thicker than blood" as his motto.

He rarely saw his former classmates from Special Ed. They were more isolated on the high school campus, in a collection of modular buildings by the practice fields. Some of them were in a life skills program that was held across town at the Recreation Center.

Lulu's eyes grew more sharp and realistic. She was able to fit an art class into her schedule each semester. By the winter of her sophomore year, she was finally satisfied with her portraits of her Special Ed colleagues, though she felt as though their stories could be made more explicit. If they were ever displayed, she wasn't going to be there all the time to explain who they were and what they fought. And she didn't want to assume anyone would read whatever description of the collection was posted in the space where they hung.

So she layered the portraits over a montage of fictionalized paperwork that communicated each subject's challenges. For some it was failed spelling tests, every word drastically misspelled, or math tests with wild guesses scribbled in response to the most simple equations. For others it was a page from an IEP that listed their hurdles, or a psychiatric evaluation.

After she composed the documents in the background, she experimented with making the tests, plans, and evaluations more visible by fading out the foreground, the faces becoming nearly transparent so that the forms behind their features overwhelmed their expression, and became what defined them.

She diluted everything but their eyes. The rest of their face was an impression, barely perceptible in front of the papers, but their eyes remained, looking to be seen.

The brick-sidewalked section of downtown with tasting rooms and restaurants also had an art gallery, where the owner reserved some space for art students from the local schools. Usually the space hosted individual pieces from a variety of students, but on occasion a student was granted a show of their own. By the spring of her junior year, Lulu's work reached a point where her collection earned a solo.

When the display was ready, she posed for a photograph in front of her corner to promote the show in both the school and local news. The owner of the gallery helped her design a postcard featuring some of the paintings and the name of the show, *Those Kids*. They made hundreds of copies and she distributed them around town.

She didn't give one to Field.

She didn't have to.

He went to the gallery when he thought hardly anybody would be there, on a weekday in the middle of its run. The wrestling team had a light workout scheduled, and he was done not long after school. The gallery owner recognized him.

"The wrestling star is an art lover?"

"I know the artist," he said.

"She's a sweet girl."

"She is."

"Usually I'd say 'let me know if you have any questions,' but I guess you can ask her next time you see her."

"Next time," he nodded.

He looked over at the collection, at all the eyes of his childhood classmates.

"Enjoy," the owner said.

"I will," he replied, though he wasn't sure he would, and wondered if that doubt came across in his voice.

He recognized everyone, despite Lulu's style. The way their faces faded into the paperwork made them even more apparent to Field, like spirits haunting him. He remembered the noises they made, their gestures, whether they were the type who smiled all the time, or who never smiled at all. He knew who was big and who was small in person, the kind of thing you can't know by looking in the eyes of a portrait. He remembered their parents, the ones who did their best to be cheerful when they had to come to a school event, the ones who tried to get in and out as discreetly as possible, and the ones who were invisible, and relied on the aides and bus drivers to keep them so.

He wasn't that far removed from them. Not a great deal of time had passed, just a great deal of change. Chemical reactions mattered more than calendars or clocks. He was now part of the majority, but on the low end of it. Without his physical gifts, he would be as nameless and faceless as his old friends hanging on the wall. He looked for a painting of himself, but Lulu didn't include him.

He called his girlfriend on the phone Gonzo had given him. She was the prettiest girl in school, according to many. He asked if she wanted to meet for an ice cream or coffee. She still had homework to do, and had taken off her makeup. He understood, told her so, then hung up and stood in the middle of Lulu's work.

The eyes in a painting usually seem to follow us, he thought, but as he walked out from the center of all his old friends' eyes, they seemed to ignore him. They stared straight ahead, avoiding contact, like most of them had in real life.

He tracked down Lulu between classes the next day and asked her how she did that, how she painted eyes that avoided eye contact.

"I didn't mean to," she said. "You're just seeing things."

"You're a good artist then, right?"

"I don't know if I should agree with you. That would be bragging."

"Making people see things is what you're supposed to do."

"I just draw. Then paint."

"Well, you're good at it. Great."

She lifted her chin in appreciation and he nodded back for lack of anything else to say. He was afraid the silence further increased the distance between where they stood and their childhood devotion.

She looked around and appeared to notice something, so he followed her lead.

People were smirking and whispering to each other as they saw the two of them speaking, people who didn't know them in elementary school, or didn't remember them. He didn't want Lulu to think he was ending their conversation due to the verdicts of the small juries passing by, but he still wasn't sure what to say.

"You should come to a meet sometime," he said. "Well, sometime next year. Season's over."

"I know."

He shook his head, admonishing himself.

"It's like wrestling is the only thing I can talk about."

"I've come to a bunch already," she smiled faintly.

"I'm sorry I didn't notice."

"There's a lot of people there."

He smiled back, his even more feeble than hers, but their smiles fed off each other and grew.

The bell rang.

"Great show," he said.

"Great season," she said.

And they went their separate ways for another four months.

I forget sometimes how different our perceptions of time are when we are young compared to when we are old, even though I'm surrounded by young people all the time. A year is a milestone to the kids I work with. A year is a reminder to me. That's my excuse for why I didn't take a more active role in convincing Field and Lulu to reconnect until the start of their senior year. And by "a more active role", I mean off-handed suggestions. The kids are like puppies in elementary school, ready to respond to any command, but then they grow into cats. I can't make suggestions, I can only hope to guide them toward a self-realization. Plus I didn't have any more official meetings with Field, only Lulu. I had to stage chance meetings with him to plant my subliminal messages.

He looked for her in the stands at his meets during his final season.

When he would find her, he resisted the urge to wave. He had waved at his sister during his first meet freshman year, and the head coach told him to never to do it again.

"You're not riding the short bus anymore," he cracked in front of the other wrestlers, whose stifled laughter sounded like a herd of elephants keeping an anxious eye on some nearby hyenas.

Aside from being unable to wave, he didn't get a chance to tell Lulu how comforting he found her presence in a mosaic of hysterical faces. She spent her senior year as a teacher's assistant in the Special Ed classes, and devoted most of her time to that isolated perimeter of the campus.

On the rare occasions he saw her, it was in passing, and he was always in the company of some teammates or his girlfriend. Lulu would avoid eye contact as they passed, so it was difficult for Field to exchange any sort of greeting without drawing more attention to her than she wanted. When he did insist on talking to her, however briefly and regarding the shallowest of topics, the people he was with were respectful enough in the moment, but their curiosity would lead to questions later on at a party or hanging out after school.

"So you were one of them?"

"You and that girl were like their king and queen?"

"How did you, like, graduate, or whatever you call it?"

Field didn't know what to call it, either, and knew even less how it happened.

Sometimes he said he matured, came through puberty more focused. Other times he felt like wrestling was the correct response, that he was moved over because it was either illegal or awkward to put someone from "the short bus" on a team. He wasn't familiar with the law, and wasn't interested in following up, as neither reason was particularly encouraging. He was grateful, but how much so depended on how much he was struggling in the mainstream. Winning a match and hearing the roar was one thing, working with a tutor just to pull a charitable "D" was another. Being with the prettiest girl in school was nice, being teased with the possibility of college was cruel.

"So you were like the fastest slow kid in elementary school," a teammate suggested.

"I guess you could say that."

"Or maybe the slowest fast kid," said another.

"That's what I am now."

He felt as though he was dashing the dreams of everyone around him each time a coach sent to recruit him would have to deal with the academic realities of his situation. There was no way around his challenges, at least not for a sport that doesn't generate piles of money. He attended a Junior Olympic program, which introduced him to another level he was unable to quite reach, so the recruitment visits stopped by his senior year, and he was able to simply play his sport and not provoke anymore fantasies.

He wondered about Lulu's plans. He snuck in a question about college after one of their chance hellos as he walked by her with his girlfriend.

"I'm going to a small private college in Arizona," she said.

"Wow!" he was happy for her. "Are you going to study art?"

"I'm going to work with Special Needs kids."

"Wow!" he said again.

"Wow," his girlfriend impersonated him badly.

Lulu looked down.

"It's really great she's going to college," he snapped at his girlfriend.

"I'm not making fun of her," she said. "Can't you think of something to say besides 'Wow'?"

Field was relieved. He laughed at himself.

Now it was Lulu who looked ready to snap.

Field noticed, and ushered his girlfriend along.

"Congratulations, Lulu," he said.

"Congratulations," his girlfriend added, attaching a homecoming queen acceptance smile.

Lulu tried to match her smile and quickly gave up as they moved on.

He thought that might be the last interaction they had until graduation, when he hoped her family would approach him with hugs and "felicidades."

But she was at the prom.

Lulu had never been to one before. She came with two of the more severe boys in the Special Ed program. Field remembered one of them from elementary school. He used to make a lot of grunting noises, and though he didn't anymore, he appeared to be making them inside his head.

She posed arm-in-arm with the two boys for their official prom photo. Field watched from his vantage several couples deep in the line waiting their turn. The girl in front of him leaned into her date and muttered, "Think they're gonna have a threesome later?"

If a boy had said it, he might have punched him. Instead he simmered. At least his girlfriend didn't laugh at the joke. Maybe she didn't hear it. He was hoping to have as much fun with her as possible before she went away on a trip to Europe after graduation, then started college on the east coast. Having fun was becoming more difficult with their paths in front of them pointing in such different directions. He was surprised she stuck with him after it became common knowledge that he would not be able to parlay his local stardom into anything of note beyond their valley. He preferred to think of her faithfulness as a sign that she truly liked him, not his local celebrity. Even if that was the case, the ticking clock was applying its pressure.

The time arrived to pose for their picture. The flash blinded him for a moment, and as he blinked his eyes in recovery, Field half-expected everything to have disappeared when he was able to try and see them again.

They said very little to each other, and danced sporadically. For the most part they stood to the side, in corners, facing forward, she leaning back into him, Field with his arms around her, like in the photo they had taken, and they watched the night pass by. Every so often a fast, catchy song that captured some of the class's memories would inspire everyone to rush the dance floor and sing along to the anthem, and they would join them. But when the song was over, Field and his girlfriend would retreat to the melancholy re-enactment of their prom picture.

During one of their spasms onto the dance floor, Field saw Lulu at a far-off table with her two guests. The song meant nothing to them. Their experience had a different soundtrack.

A slow song came on and chased off half the couples, including Field and his girlfriend. If they were going to hold each other close, they seemed to have agreed, no need to do so in front of everyone.

"You want to get out of here?" she asked before they reached their latest corner.

She may have said it suggestively, but Field would not have noticed. He was too concerned with time.

"Is it that late already?"

"This is probably the last song."

He looked over at Lulu and the boys. He thought of asking her to dance, but had been in the mainstream long enough to feel the current pull him back when he tried to make a move in her direction.

"Okay," he answered his girlfriend. "I just need to go to the bathroom."

"I'll see you outside," she kissed him.

After he washed his hands, he stood over the sink and watched the water circle down the drain. He cursed himself, pulled a sheet from the paper towel dispenser, and dried off. He wadded the paper into a ball and raised his arm to throw it into the bin overflowing with discarded sheets, but froze before following through.

He lowered his arm and stared at the damp, ragged heap. The music was just audible through the walls, the last song of the last prom. He tossed his small contribution into the collection and scrambled to pull a bunch of fresh towels from the dispenser.

The walk to Lulu's table suddenly felt so smooth, as though gliding along with the current rather than against it. She couldn't see him coming from the angle he took, which was by design and helped ease his approach. He suffered a last-second clench of doubt, but took comfort in the bounty of wadded-up paper towels in his arms.

She looked up, saw him bearing his industrial bouquet, and put her hand over her mouth.

"May I have this dance?" he asked.

She nodded, unable to speak.

He realized he had made such a large arrangement that both hands were occupied. He looked for a place to put them, shrugged, and let them fall to the floor as he reached out to her.

Her guests anxiously surveyed the litter.

She giggled and took his hand.

"I'm not even muddy," she said as they found a clear space to dance.

Field couldn't think of anything to say, as had so often been the case when he found himself in Lulu's presence during high school, but that didn't seem to matter now. Saying nothing felt like the right thing to do. There was only a minute left in the song, but the song was an excuse to hug her, and a hug that lasts for a minute is nice and long. Longer than they had ever hugged in elementary school before someone would yell "safe hands", and longer than we were allowed to hug them as their educators and counselors. Certainly longer than anyone in his family had hugged him. She was more used to affection, and so more comfortable when the song ended.

He reverted back to desperation over what to say. Within seconds, though, Lulu's eyes sprung from contentment to surprise. Field felt someone tapping his arm. He looked over to find Lulu's two guests presenting him with his pile of paper towels, accompanied by Lulu's laughter.

"Thanks, guys," Field smiled.

"You made a mess," one of them said, the one he recalled from elementary school.

"I did," Field agreed and glanced at Lulu.

"You made a mess," he repeated.

"Don't worry, Gage," Lulu calmed him. ""He'll throw them away on his way out."

"Gage," Field stretched the name with recognition as he took the pile from him. "How have you been?"

Gage shrugged his shoulders.

"Getting by?" Lulu offered a possible translation.

He shrugged his shoulders again.

"Thanks for helping me clean up," Field almost reached out to put a hand on his shoulder, but remembered that probably wouldn't go well.

Instead he looked at Lulu, who looked back at him.

That's all they did.

That's all they did for the last month of high school. They stayed in their respective corners, but they would see each other from a distance and smile.

Even after the graduation ceremony, when her parents rushed to congratulate him as he hoped they would, he and Lulu simply hugged. Not for as long as they did at the prom, under the guise of a slow dance, but there may as well have been music playing.

# CHAPTER FIVE: LIFE

Field stood in the irrigation aisle at the home improvement store, looking through the space between the shelves at the stairs that led up to Gonzo's office. Yadier was in the store again, and Field was curious if he was paying Gonzo another visit. He was always grateful for the kindness Yadi extended him when he was still a middle schooler training with the team and Yadi was a senior.

The first few times Field had run into Yadier, he assumed he was there to shop for supplies like anyone else, but he noticed that Yadier tended to leave empty-handed. One of those times, Field was in the nursery loading one-gallon pots of daisies onto the outside display. Yadier was about to cross into the parking lot, and Field hailed him.

"Can I help you find something, Yadi?"

"I'm good, Field. Thanks!"

Field waved and got back to work, his curiosity piqued.

"Excuse me," a voice interrupted Field's surveillance of Gonzo's office.

"Oh," Field clocked his attention back in. "Yes, sir."

"Do you have a half-inch drip line?" asked a man who smelled of top soil and wore a landscaping company cap and shirt soiled with the source of the scent. "No more on the shelf."

"I'll check, sir," Field reached for the radio on his hip.

The man looked around for something to pretend to look at while Field made his call.

"Gonzo?"

"Yeah, Field?"

"Do we have any half-inch dripline in back?"

"Let me check."

There was a pause and Field heard Gonzo tap on his keyboard, with an occasional emphatic strike of the "enter" key that served as an audio exclamation point. The customer would glance over every time he heard the punctuation, expecting it led to an answer. Field would nod at him.

"It says here we do," Gonzo eventually replied.

Field and the customer exchanged smiles.

"You in irrigation?" Gonzo asked.

"Yup."

"I'll send Mike over with some."

"Excellent," Field started to holster the radio.

"Oh, and Field?" Gonzo's voice stopped him.

"Yes?" he drew the radio back up.

"Could you come to my office when you get a chance?"

"Sure."

"See you then."

Field lowered the radio and his service smile.

"You get a raise?" the customer joked.

"Well, it has been over a year," Field considered the possibility. "And they're raising my rent. The timing would be great."

"You go, then," the customer waved him ahead. "I wait for Mike. Is Mike, right?"

"Yes," Field considered the other possibilities besides a raise. "It's Mike."

He drifted toward the office while sifting through recollections of Gonzo being upset with him as an employee. He had never been terribly angry, but did have to talk to him every so often about being a bit more responsive to customer needs. Field had a tendency to wander the aisles and delight in some of the more precise items. The day he happened upon a stud finder, he spent time pressing it against any patch of exposed wall he could find, searching for signals. As he found them, he traced the pattern on how close together they were, or far apart, and stepped back to imagine what the frame of the building looked like underneath the walls, until Gonzo interrupted his visualization and asked him to head over the lumber department and load some fence posts into a customer's pickup. He loved to take stock of the garden statues and predict which ones would sell the most, though his tastes never seemed to align with the public's.

"Field!" Gonzo bellowed good-naturedly as he entered his office after a gentle tap on the door that was ajar.

Yadi sat in the chair on the opposite side of his desk.

"Close it behind you," Gonzo gestured to the door.

He and Yadi both stood as Field followed orders.

"You remember Yadi?"

Field stepped forward to shake his hand.

"I sure do."

"He's the only one," Yadi joked as he took up Field on his handshake. "Unlike this guy."

Yadi raised Field's hand as if declaring him a winner.

"Everybody remembers the champ," he grinned, then playfully tapped Field in the stomach with his other hand.

Field instinctively doubled over, then laughed along with the two of them at their reaction. As the laughter subsided, Gonzo suggested everyone sit down. Yadi grabbed a chair from the back of the room and dragged it next to his, gesturing for Field sit by him as Gonzo picked up the conversation where they left off.

"They just don't come up to you like they used to, eh Field?" he said. "Like it's embarrassing or something that you work here. What's wrong with working at the home store, huh? The do-it-yourself store?"

"Nothing," Field shrugged.

"Do It Yourself. That's what America is all about. More people should work at a place like this."

"Where do you work, Yadi?" Field asked.

The men laughed again.

"How do you do that?" Gonzo asked Field.

"Do what?"

"Nail someone without even trying to nail them."

"It's the sincerity," Yadi said.

"You mean what you say," Gonzo agreed. "When you joke, it's no joke. That's why it cuts to the bone."

"Should I not have asked?" Field looked apologetically at Yadi.

"It's fine," Yadi assured him.

"This time," Gonzo chuckled.

"I'm involved in real estate," Yadi finally answered the question.

"Wow," Field said. "Have I seen your name on one of those signs in front of a house?"

"He buys investment properties," Gonzo said on Yadi's behalf. "Over in the central valley."

"The coastal valley is a bit out of my price range," Yadi explained.

"For now," Gonzo smiled.

"What's an investment property?" Field asked.

"Rentals," Yadi answered. "Apartment buildings, condos, an occasional house."

"Sounds great, Yadi."

"I like it. Hard work. Risky."

"It's like playing a sport," Gonzo said. "It's like wrestling."

"Well, then, I'm sure you're good at it," Field said. "Does this have anything to do with why you called me in, Coach?"

"There it is," Yadi motioned. "The sincerity."

"You called it, Yadi," Gonzo said. "And you guessed it, Field."

"Gonzo sold appliances to some of my tenants."

"Not sure if 'sold' is the right word."

"We cut some sweet deals," Yadi agreed. "Way better than they could get at the same store over on their side of the hill."

"And even then, practically giving the stuff away, we get people slacking off on the payments."

"That's too bad," Field said.

"Especially since this is all off the books," Gonzo said. "We can't hire any bill collectors."

"Off the books?" Field was curious.

"These are farm workers," Yadi defended the practice. "They can barely make rent. There isn't a deal we could make through any credit company that they could afford. We have to go under the table for them to have any chance at a better life."

"I use products that were dented or scratched on delivery to the store, and the display models once they're taken off the floor."

"That's a good idea," said Field.

"Glad you think so, champ," Gonzo grinned. "But we still have this problem with the deadbeats."

"We thought you might be able to help."

"What can I do?"

"Yadi is too close to them," Gonzo said. "I mean, they respect him, but he was in a lower weight class. He was a scrapper. They wouldn't know he was a great wrestler unless they asked, or he told them."

"And what's more pathetic than some old jock telling stories about the glory days?" Yadi chuckled.

"But you, my son," Gonzo wagged a finger at Field. "People know what you're capable of on sight."

Field processed what Gonzo said.

"I don't think anybody in the next valley will recognize me."

Gonzo suppressed a smile.

"Probably not," he agreed. "But that's not what I'm talking about."

"You're a big dude," Yadi jumped on the chance to lighten the tone. "Huge, bro. Just stand there and look scary and boom! They start throwin' the money at us."

"No more late payments," Gonzo clarified.

"Do I look scary?"

"Not to us," Yadi said. "Not to anyone who knows you. But like you said, they don't know you out there."

"And I scare people who don't know me?"

"No," Gonzo assured him. "Not under normal circumstances. Just walking down the street, or waiting in line, ordering some food. But this will be different. Yadi will be collecting money they owe. They're already uncomfortable. He does the talking, you stand behind him with a serious look on your face."

"Don't smile," Yadi teased.

"I see," Field bowed his head.

"Easy money," Yadi pitched.

"Double per hour what you make here at the store," Gonzo pressed.

"Really?" Field glanced up.

"Ah," Yadi held the word like a long note in a song. "Now we've got his attention."

"Most of the time the drive will take longer than the job itself," Gonzo continued to build their case.

"What do I do with myself the rest of the time?"

Gonzo started to strain at having to explain every conceivable angle.

"You can keep your job here at the store," he almost sighed. "In fact, I'd prefer it that way. This is a side hustle."

"You're a good kid," Yadi said. "We're not asking you to do anything that's not you. We're just putting on a show."

Field shifted in his chair.

"Why don't you think about it," Gonzo suggested.

He took out a couple of twenty dollars bills and slid them across the desk.

"Clock out early, have a big lunch, get some rest. Let me know tomorrow."

Field didn't take the bills right away. Gonzo and Yadier assured him it was okay, that he was being reimbursed for time lost at work so he could ponder his future.

He wasn't hungry, but he didn't want to go to his apartment. He went to the coffee house where people dressed nicely and sounded smart, hoping their conversations would rub off on him, that their language would help him construct an argument for why he should or should not take the offer.

I wish he had spoken with me. We didn't have our reunion until later, by accident, and until that happened, he felt as though my counsel was no longer an option since he was no longer in school. I could have reached out. I wish that, too. The largest influences in his decision ended up being his apartment and his car.

Any inspiration he may have gathered from eavesdropping in the upscale coffee house was likely sapped by hoping his car would start on the first turn of the ignition, and pulling into a parking space that faced one of the milky windows of his splintered apartment building.

Every pristine new neighborhood that was developed in stride with the valley's growing allure to tourists and retirees seemed to expose the native structures as the afterthoughts they often were, built for shelter rather than prestige in an era when nobody imagined farming would move from basic need to trendy amenity, at least in certain areas dedicated to certain crops.

The next valley, farther away from shore, was marked by staple crops that hugged the ground, main courses and side dishes, rather than the glamorous products that hung from the trees and vines of the western valley that made everything taste better. If the two valleys were neighborhoods, the inland valley would be the one on the wrong side of the tracks, according to the old expression. It rarely had any visitors who weren't associated with the business of what grew. Oak trees that used the grassy hillsides as platforms on which to strike their poses along the coastal landscape faded as the air distanced itself from the Pacific, leaving the interior hillsides mostly bare. The towns achieved the minimum required of them, places to sleep and eat.

Yadier would drive on their trips inward. His enormous pickup truck always shined as though he had just driven it off the lot. They would pass a large building on one of the highest hills between the two valleys, several peaks away from the highway. It looked like a metal barn that had been painted brown so it wouldn't reflect the sun, but the grain elevator attached to it looked more like a tower.

"It is a tower," Yadi explained when Field wondered aloud at what the building was. "The state used to pay a ranger to sit in it during fire season to keep an eye out for smoke. You can see both valleys from up there."

"They don't use it anymore?"

"They realized spotting a fire isn't the hard part," Yadi said. "It's fighting it. So they put that money into a bigger crew."

Everyone they visited knew Yadi, and like everyone else who knew him, they seemed to enjoy his company, even though he was there to collect money from them. They would update him up on what had been going on since his last visit. Field didn't understand most of their conversations, as they spoke Spanish to each other. He was never introduced to anyone, either. Yadi would occasionally gesture toward him as he spoke with a client, but the idea was to keep Field on the outskirts of the meetings, to be more of a presence than a person.

He understood why Yadi and Gonzo would prefer such an arrangement, but other parts of their trips confused him. Some of the houses looked like they weren't even hooked up to a source of electricity. They were shacks with glass in about half the windows, cardboard in the other half.

"Generators," Yadi explained. "They use generators to run the appliances."

"It seems like they could use a lot of other things first."

Yadi shrugged.

"They lived in worse places before they came here. Now add a washing machine. Pretty sweet, from their point of view."

Sometimes they would eat lunch at the buffet of a casino on an Indian Reservation. The casino rose above the surrounding neighborhood like a fortress, as though the homes on the perimeter were an encamped army. The houses were about as sturdy as tents, with moldy couches on dried front lawns, while the driveway of the casino circled around a fountain that spewed water in a dozen different directions. Field liked the buffet, as it offered a lot of food for a small price, but he didn't like having to get there by walking through the cigarette smoke that saturated the gaming floor. Yadi always wanted to play blackjack on their way out, so Field was stuck on the floor that much longer, trying to breathe out for longer stretches than he breathed in. Fortunately Yadi never played for very long, but then they'd have to stop at the window because he always bought way more chips than he needed and had to cash them in on his way out.

"Why don't you just buy what you need?" Field finally asked.

"I want to look like a big shot when I sit at the table," he smiled.

Yadi always paid him after a trip to the casino, which in addition to lunch, made the smoke more bearable.

Gonzo wasn't kidding. The money was great.

He had never seen a one-hundred dollar bill before he started working the valley. Yadi would hand him several at a time. Field didn't spend any of the bills for the first few months on the job. He collected them in a bundle that he bound with a rubber band and put inside his old Paw Patrol lunchbox from elementary school. The stack of hundreds would make him giggle as much as the cartoons on his lunchbox would when he was a kid. He used his paycheck from the home improvement store to scrape by, while the stack of cash remained a source of wonder.

And for those first few months, it was also as easy as Gonzo said it would be.

He really was paid to ride in the car with Yadi and stand nearby while business transpired. It was like being a security guard at a slow event, only nobody ever asked him for directions, and the only one he was supposed to help was Yadi. He never seriously considered himself a bodyguard, since he never imagined Yadi needing protection, only backup. Besides, none of the customers were at all threatening. There were a couple of big men, but they had kind faces, and were very deferential toward Yadi.

"How long are you gonna stay in that horrible apartment building?" Yadi asked him one afternoon as they dropped into the eastern valley after Field's morning shift at the store. They were heading to one of the towns which hosted one of the prisons. Field watched the guard towers and walls through the haze created by speeding past the chain link fence at ninety miles per hour.

"I don't know," Field shrugged.

"And that car," Yadi shuddered. "Damn."

"I'm not sure what to buy first."

"What would make you happiest?"

"I don't like going to my apartment," Field thought aloud. "It makes me sad. But my car makes me nervous."

"So what's more important? Getting rid of the sadness? Or the nerves?"

"The people we collect from, their places make me sad, too."

"Hey," Yadi protested. "Some of those are my buildings."

"I didn't mean yours..."

"I'm kidding," Yadi chuckled. "They're all shitty. I know it."

"What I mean is that maybe I'm stuck with the sad part."

Yadi processed Field's logic.

"So a car, then?" he concluded.

"I guess so," Field still didn't seem certain.

"I know a guy."

"You always do."

"Connections, man," Yadi backhanded Field's arm. "The key to life."

They made it past the prison and slowed into the town, which was filled with houses like the ones around the casino, only without the casino. They turned onto a street behind a shopping center where it was hard to tell which stores were still in business and which ones had given up. Their destination turned out to be an apartment building that would have reminded Yadi to ask Field if he was planning on moving out of his, if he hadn't asked already. It was worse than the houses, because it was just as bad, but much bigger. There were two stories of doors facing the elements without a fresh coat of paint since its days as a cut-rate motel.

"This could get uncomfortable," Yadi said as he cut the engine.

Field looked at him for further explanation.

"This guy is way behind," he explained. "Way behind. And shows no interest in catching up. You may have to earn your money today."

Field tried to nod, but his head barely moved.

Yadi laughed.

"Just follow my lead, champ."

They walked up one of the exterior staircases that flanked each end of the dwelling to the second story balcony. A smell climbed along with them, like the back of a restaurant: cooking oil, grease, and leftovers. Yadi led the way to a door in the midsection. He glanced at Field.

"Neighbors on each side," he noted. "Let's keep this as quiet as possible."

He knocked.

"Look mean," he reminded him.

A woman answered. She was older, but her exact age was difficult to gauge thanks to a career in the sun. She looked frightened.

Yadi addressed her in Spanish. Unlike most of the previous interactions Field had witnessed between Yadi and the customers, his words did not comfort her. She appeared even more frightened as she let them in.

Yadi told her to sit down. Field understood that much, maybe because she sat down right after he gave her the command. She also kept her eyes down. He proceeded to berate her until she started to cry. He leaned in closer to her, and started whispering in her ear, but not to calm her down. It was an intense whisper. While he was in her ear, he looked back at Field, and gestured toward him. He grabbed her chin and forced her to look up at him as well.

Field stared back at her and forgot he was supposed to look intimidating. Yadi gave him some visual directions. He snarled and furled his brows. Maybe he was just mad at Field. It didn't matter, because the woman never really looked at him. She instead looked sideways as far as she could.

Yadi let her go and stood before her. He spoke to her in a more measured tone, but sounded like he could still uncoil at any moment. He turned to exit, tapping Field on the way, who followed him and closed the door behind them.

Yadi headed for the staircase on the opposite end of the balcony. He assessed the property as they walked. Nobody was visible.

"Good," he said as they descended. "I was afraid I raised my voice too much."

He sounded familiar again, as though he had been playing a character in the woman's apartment.

"You need to work on your mean mug, by the way," he continued. "We're lucky she was too scared to look at you. If you want to try going against type, go with a smile. That could really freak people out. But you can't look confused."

Field waited until they were in Yadi's truck before speaking.

"You said it was a guy."

"It is. That's his wife."

"Where was he?"

"He's working. Out in the fields."

"And you knew that?"

"He's not listening to us. Maybe he'll listen to her."

Yadi backed out of his parking space and proceeded back out onto the road while Field tried to make sense of the last five minutes.

"All this for a washing machine?" he finally asked.

Yadi smiled. He seemed to agree that it was absurd, but he offered an explanation anyway.

"It's the principle," he said. "And I don't mean the principal balance. You know, before interest payments kick in?"

Field didn't get it, but wasn't ready to joke about the situation even if he did.

Yadi sighed.

"The system doesn't work if people don't keep their word. We might as well just give them the stuff."

"Why don't we?"

"We?" Yadi playfully reared back. "So you're part of the decision-making process now? You ride shotgun for a few months and you're ready for a seat at the table?"

"Why does Gonzo have to buy the appliances?" Field sincerely considered the possibility. "Can't he convince the company to donate them, since they're dinged up and all?"

He waited for Yadi to fire back some reason why his idea wasn't possible, or some frisky insult, but instead he drove in silence. Field wondered if he had said something wrong, and was about to ask him if that was the case when Yadi finally spoke.

"You're a good man, Field."

Field was grateful for the compliment, but it sounded odd. Nobody had ever referred to him as a man before. He thanked him.

"Don't thank me," he said. "Don't change."

They visited a couple more customers without incident before proceeding back to the main highway which took them on their home stretch.

The setting sun didn't pull the heat down with it in the eastern valley, but as they passed the abandoned ranger station that marked their passage from east to west, they could feel the evening temperature drop through the open windows as they drew closer to the ocean. The drive into comfort reminded him of how grateful he was to live there.

He wondered if it was necessary to pick on those who didn't in order to stay.

Yadi made some wrong turns when they reached town.

"Do we have errands to run?" Field asked.

"Nope. I'm taking you home."

"But this isn't the way."

Yadi grinned and kept driving. As his grin faded, he sped up.

"I wish you had asked me that five minutes later," he said. "The timing would have been perfect. Anyway…"

He pulled into one of the new developments that had the word "vineyard" in its name, which was spelled out in wrought iron by the entrance. Gently winding streets meandered through houses that looked like they had the ability to choose who lived in them. After a few slow curves, they came to a condominium complex that was as judgmental as the houses.

"Welcome to your new home," Yadi announced as they pulled to a stop in front.

"What?"

"Not the whole thing, of course, but that corner unit on the second floor."

"Are you kidding?"

"Gonzo paid the deposit. All you need to do is pay the rent."

"This is…"

"Words escape you. I get it. Come on, let's check it out."

They bounded up the stairs and Yadi presented him with the key. Field had never been inside a new home before.

"It's small, but it's clean," Yadi narrated as they toured the space. "I'm not sure if anyone lived in it before you. If they did, they didn't spend much time here."

Field smelled wood and fresh carpet, a faint scent of paint, but nothing human.

"It's beautiful," he said.

"That's a relief," Yadi quipped. "When you said you were thinking of getting a car before a new place to live, I was afraid you'd be disappointed."

Field laughed.

"No way," he said as he continued to gaze at his new home. "No way."

Field turned to face Yadi.

"Thank you."

"Thank Gonzo," he shrugged. "He did most of the work. I just found the place."

"I will."

"You can thank me for the car later."

"My goodness," Field shook his head in disbelief.

"You deserve it," Yadi assured him. "You've been through a lot."

Field kept shaking his head, staving off tears.

"Can I help you bring your stuff over?" Yadi asked.

"No," Field fended off his emotions enough to respond.

"You sure? I'm dropping you off at your old place, anyway."

"I don't have much."

Yadi put a hand on his shoulder.

"Don't forget what I said," he told him. "You're a good man. You deserve this."

He squeezed Field's shoulder before using the same hand to gesture toward the door.

"Now let's clear you out of that old dump."

Field wasn't simply being polite. He really didn't have much. All he needed was a single trip between his old and new home.

Besides a week's worth of clothes, his bathroom supplies, and a futon mattress he rolled up off the floor, the only item he carried with him was a clock radio. Gonzo used to give them out to the Employees of the Month before cell phones dictated time. He still had a box of clock radios in his office, and Field asked for one when Gonzo hired him at the home improvement store. Gonzo said he could have the whole box if wanted, but Field just needed a replacement for his brother's CD player in the room they shared at their mother's house. He never did see his brother use it, and hardly saw his brother for that matter, so he probably could have taken the CD player with him when he left. But he was certain his brother would come for it when he finally noticed it was gone, and Field wanted nothing to do with his family once he moved out.

At first he missed being able to listen to his *Symphony of the Ocean* CD when he needed to relax, but in exploring the radio dial he discovered a classical music station that played real symphony music. He found it just as relaxing as the whale calls and synthesizers, and they hardly ever played any commercials since the selections were so long. He grew familiar with the names of the composers, but could never remember the name of a given piece. There were too many layers, whether it was a concerto or sonata or symphony, what number it was, and what key it was in. But he wasn't looking to be an authority. He wanted to relax.

He lied on his futon in his new bedroom and listened to the tinny sound of his clock radio play beautiful music. It soothed him as usual, but then he thought about why he had relied on the music before. He needed to know the taunts, stares, and whispers would go away some day. He needed to know that the bully was motivated by self-hatred. He needed to know he would find his place in the world.

He was no longer the bullied. He was the bully.

He wondered if that was his place in the world.

The orchestra played on.

# CHAPTER SIX: DECISIONS

The billboards that encouraged travelers to exit and spend their money referred to it as "The Crossroads of The Valley", and indeed it stood at the intersection of two highways. You could proceed north or south to one of the large metro areas, head east to the mountains, or west to wine country. There was no hotel at The Crossroads, just a collection of eateries and gift shops disguised as an old western town, nestled behind the gas stations and fast food that stood at the forefront of the on-ramps and off-ramps.

Yadi like the barbeque they served at the place between the ice cream stand and the gift shop specializing in sculptures made of old farm implements, so sometimes they would stop there for lunch during a collection run. Field liked it, too, and noticed they tended to stop for barbeque after the more tense visits, which had become more frequent since the incident with the customer's wife.

Field even had to wrestle a man to the ground during one exchange.

It happened in the dusty center court of a square of bungalows, as if they were wrestling inside a ring. The man was bigger than either of them, and more belligerent than any customer they had visited. He clearly thought his size and aggression would intimidate the intimidators, but when he made a move on Yadi, those self-perceived advantages were easy to use against him. Field had him face-down in the dirt and immobilized within seconds. He felt no remorse, as he experienced with the smaller and meeker customers. The outdoor wrestling match felt more fair. In addition to his nature, the big man had made the first move.

When Yadi grumbled something into the fallen giant's ear and took some cash out of his wallet, Field's sense of justice waned. They had struck first after all, on behalf of Gonzo.

"You legend is growing," Yadi said as they pulled into a parking spot a several swinging doors down from The Crossroads BBQ.

"My legend?"

"That last guy we visited asked if you were the gringo who took down Victor."

"The big dude from the bungalows a couple weeks ago?"

"I said 'Who else would it be?', and he handed the money right over."

Yadi chuckled as he set the emergency brake.

"He used to give me a lot of trouble," he continued.

"Victor?"

"No, that little chingada who got your message."

"You could take any of these guys," Field wasn't sure whether he wanted to be modest or lay the groundwork for his resignation. "Including Victor. He's big and sloppy."

"I know, but I couldn't do it alone. I need a spotter in case someone thinks of moving in. Like those people who wear costumes at Disneyland. There's Mickey Mouse, and his shadow, ready to jump in if someone gets crazy."

"Really?"

"Sure. Nobody notices because they're too busy trying to take a picture with Mickey."

"I've never been there."

"You should go sometime," Yadi started to get out of the truck. "Now that you're making some real money."

Field followed him out.

"So you're Mickey Mouse and I'm the spotter," he caught up.

"You got it," Yadi laughed.

"I feel like I'm the one wearing a costume," Field said somewhat to himself.

"Try being this charming this often," Yadi mirrored his self-reflection.

The Crossroads BBQ was a meat mall, two stories high, all the smokers and grills visible behind glass walls. The wooden walls were hung with black and white photographs of humble barbeque joints from the swampiest and driest corners of the country.

Field and Yadi stood silently in line and remained quiet during their meal for the most part, as the high-volume hubbub made having a conversation tiring.

A stocky man from one of the grill stations came over and greeted Yadi in Spanish. Their loud exchange suited the atmosphere. Field tensed up with wonder over whether they could ever escape their job when they were on this side of the hills.

"An old friend," Yadi notified Field between back slaps and hand gestures. "No business."

Field lightened.

They were still talking when Field finished his tri-tip sandwich, so he excused himself.

"I'll be in the gift shop."

Yadi nodded while his old friend smiled and waved.

Field bypassed the postcards and t-shirts in the shop and headed for the farm implement sculptures. He liked trying to figure out what each part used to be.

He was drawn to an owl that had two old disc blades for eyes. The previous purpose of the discs was easy enough to discern. They had gone from tilling fields to staring at customers. The feel of the eyes is what he found interesting. He rested his cheek on one of them. The surface was cool to the touch, cooler than the air in the shop. Field imagined how hot it would be if left in the sun, hotter than the air around it and the ground on which it stood, how the steel amplified whatever environment it was in.

"Sir?" a voice interrupted his revelation.

He jerked his head from the steel eye. A light blue polo shirt worn by the employees flashed in his field of vision. He apologized without making eye contact.

"Field?" the voice sounded familiar.

He focused on the employee wearing the light blue shirt.

She looked like Lulu.

He needed a moment to make sure he was out of his metal-induced trance.

"I should have known it was you," she smiled. "Do you need to 'shake the page'?"

He rushed over and hugged her off her feet, spinning around in a circle. Her legs flew into a display of tumbleweeds that had been dipped in liquid metal. A few of them rolled to the floor.

"Oops," Field put her down. "Sorry."

He gathered one of the spiky spheres and placed it back on the pile. She joined him.

"I should probably help," she said.

"You work here?"

"Yes," she briefly modeled her light blue polo shirt.

"Why?"

"Why?" she held up his question as an example of a bad question.

"I mean," Field stopped gathering tumbleweeds and stood to gather his thoughts instead, "why out here? Why aren't you home? Or do you drive all the way out here?"

"I live with my aunt and uncle. Out here."

"Oh. But what happened to college? Are you on break? I'm sorry. I'm asking too many questions. I'm just so happy to see you."

"You sure are."

She finished putting the tumbleweeds back in their place.

"Aren't you happy to see me?" he asked.

"Yes," she tried to assure him. "I'm just surprised. I wasn't expecting to see anyone from our town."

"It's not that far away."

"I guess it seems farther when you're a kid. And now we're not."

She checked her work on the display to make sure the pieces would hold.

"I drive here all the time," Field demanded her attention.

"What for?"

"Well," he didn't want to craft a lie that would be hard to remember. "I deliver appliances. I'm a delivery man."

"That's a lot of territory to cover."

"Oh, we have these special deals. Gonzo runs the program. Remember my wrestling coach?"

"Yes."

"The stores out here don't offer what we do."

"That's nice."

"It's good money. I moved out of my Mom's house. I'm in one of those nice new condominium buildings."

"Wow."

"You should come visit."

"I don't have a car. My uncle gives me a ride when he can."

"Have him drive you over. He and your aunt probably visit your Mom and Dad anyway, right?"

"His truck isn't very reliable. Plus my aunt is shy. She spent most of her life in Mexico. None of us know her very well. Mom and Dad come out here once in a while."

"What happens when your uncle can't give you a ride?"

"I have some nice co-workers."

"Maybe one of them can come with you. Make it a wine country trip."

"I don't know any of them that well. We're just work friends."

"I'm getting a new car pretty soon."

"Okay."

"What are your days off?"

"I work almost every day. I like to help out my aunt and uncle with the rent, and I like to spend as little time as possible in their place. It's not nice."

"I could meet you somewhere. Maybe here, after your shift, or on your lunch break."

"Sure. I don't have a phone, though."

"When I have a day off I'll call this gift shop and see if you're here. And if you are, I'll race over."

"In your new car."

"That's right," he swooped his fist, then thought of something. "So it might not be for a while."

Lulu smiled.

"What if you get here and my break isn't for a couple of hours?"

"I'll hang out, eat barbeque, rub my face on the sculptures. I'll do whatever it takes to see you."

She laughed before losing touch with her smile.

"I apologize if it doesn't seem like I want to see you too," she said. "I really do. All those excuses I made, they're real."

"I believe you."

Lulu looked around to see if anyone was nearby.

"I flunked out of college," she continued to look away.

Field took a deep, sad breath.

"I'm sorry, Lulu."

He stepped in to hug her, but stopped when she still wouldn't look at him. He didn't want to startle her.

"It's still fresh," she said to the distance. "I started this job when I would have started my sophomore year. I knew halfway through freshman year it was over. But being here instead of there makes it sink in."

She finally looked at him.

"I didn't move back home because I didn't want to face anyone," she explained. "Including my family. I spent the summer working a job on campus, then moved here when my scholarship was officially revoked. That's why I'm being weird."

"You're not being weird."

"Yes I am."

"Maybe a little."

"Thank you," she seemed capable of smiling. "If I felt like I was acting weird and I really wasn't, that would be even more weird. Then again, I'm relying on your judgment."

Field laughed.

"You sound so smart."

"It was the work," she sighed. "I learned so much. I felt so smart. I still do. But I can't prove it. I can't write it down, I can't share it. Not in a way that anyone understands. I know good work when I see it, but I can't do it."

"Maybe you can try again sometime."

"Still the sweetest boy," she rubbed his arm. "Even if you weren't for a while in high school."

"We weren't hanging out, that's all. Doesn't mean I was a jerk."

She put her head down and smirked up at him.

"I've done worse since then," he tried to joke, but the truth of what he said buried the effort.

"Really?" she noticed his miscalculation.

"Nothing that bad," he backpedaled. "Sometimes we have to lean on people to get them to pay their bills."

"Lean on them?"

"Scare them."

"You?" she giggled. "Scare people?"

"Yeah," Field was mildly offended.

"And not because you're taking up a big chunk of the school budget anymore, but for real? Just you, scaring people?"

Field tried not to laugh.

"You don't think I can?"

Lulu shook her head.

"Imagine you don't know me," he asked.

"I can't," she shrugged.

"Try."

"That's simply not possible."

She smiled at him.

It was the best he had felt since graduation, and he told her so.

"Getting the new condo was close," he realized out loud. "But this is still the best."

"Yes!" she pumped her fist. "Eat it, condo!"

Her celebration was a bit too loud, prompting her manager to peer down the aisle.

"Sorry, Celeste!" she called out to her.

Celeste didn't appear to think an apology was enough.

"An old friend," Lulu gestured toward Field. "We haven't seen each other in like a year and a half."

"That's not that old," Celeste waved her off. "I have friends I haven't seen in ten years."

"Are they still friends at that point?" Lulu asked.

Celeste gave her the kind of look that usually comes with a pair of crossed arms.

"Make some plans together and wrap it up," she threw in a grin before tilting back into what she was doing before.

"I should get back to work, too," Field said. "I told Yadi where I was, but he might be waiting by the truck. You remember Yadier? He graduated before we were freshman, but he was the captain of the wrestling team when I trained with them in middle school. I must have mentioned him."

"You probably did, but I started to tune out when you'd talk about wrestling."

"What?"

"Not at first," she qualified. "But after a while it was wrestling this, wrestling that. All wrestling, all the time."

"Yeah," he admitted.

"So there's good news in that not working out. If you were still doing it, I wouldn't want to see you again."

"I'm going to see you again?" he confirmed.

"The silver lining to your shattered dream."

Field thought she looked younger than she used to, that she had grown out of looking like an old lady in miniature. She had jumped out from under that shroud and captured her true age. Her eyes were still big, but didn't seem to protrude as much. Her posture was still a bit hunched over, but spoke to the anxieties of being a struggling young adult, rather than early osteoporosis.

Yadi was indeed by his truck, but still talking to the barbeque staff member. Taking their conversation outside made Field wonder if it really was business instead of pleasure, but their tone continued to sound friendly, and their embrace as they said goodbye offered a persuasive closing argument. A cordial nod from Yadi's old friend convinced Field it was safe to bring up a new car once they were back on the road.

"You want it all, eh Field?" Yadi needled him.

"I think it would be good for all of us, for me to have a car I can trust to drive out here, you know, in case you or Gonzo need me to take care of something when you're not available."

"You make a pretty good case," Yadi smiled. "We'll use that on Gonzo if we need him to front some more cash. But we might not need it."

"Because you know a guy."

"Because I know a guy. Let's visit him."

Yadi veered onto the last exit before the highway took them up and out of the valley.

The first dry mile of the road gave way to some warehouses and lots surrounded by chain link fences which didn't appear to be necessary, as there was nothing behind them, except for the one they pulled over alongside.

Dozens of vehicles of various makes, models, and years were lined up, some with more dust on them than others. Yadi and Field stepped out of the truck and walked to the gate. A sign clung to the links that read, "Police Impound Do Not Enter".

"Rudy!" Yadi shouted past it.

A man in coveralls rose from behind one of the cars a couple of rows away.

"Got a customer for you!" Yadi stuck his thumb at Field.

Rudy grinned and came forward.

"Don't look like one of ours," he said as he arrived at the gate.

"I said 'customer', not 'convict'. We're lookin' to buy."

Rudy took out a set of keys from his pocket and used one to release the padlock that held the chain in place that coiled around the entrance. The chain slithered off and hung from the handle.

"Coffee and donuts in the lounge," Rudy muttered.

"We just ate," Field said.

Yadi and Rudy glanced at each other before Yadi brought them back to the main subject.

"Got anything with good gas mileage and a few good years left in it?"

"You know we do," Rudy led them to the aisles. "People bite off a lot more car than they can chew."

"What's up with this one?" Yadi pointed to a newish-looking compact sedan at the edge of the aisle they were heading toward.

"Just came in day before yesterday," Rudy said as they arrived at its side. "Notice the lack of dust."

"Hmm..." Yadi crossed his arms. "Too soon?"

"When was the last time anyone claimed a car around here?"

"You tell me."

"Never."

"Okay, then. How about it?"

"Sold."

"How much?"

"Two large."

"How about one-five?"

"The five hundred is for me. Deputy Dawg is gonna want more than a grand."

"Seventeen-fifty."

"More than a symbolic number above a grand."

"Aw, come one, Rudy. You're no fun anymore."

"Two is a steal. I shoulda started the bidding at three. This thing doesn't only run good, it's already been sold two times at Pete's lot. Darren wants to take it out of the rotation."

"Oh, you shouldn't have told me that."

"I gave you nothin', man," Rudy smiled. "He'd just as soon I bring it to the scrap yard. Take it or leave it."

"Fine," Yadi surrendered. "Where's the paperwork?"

Rudy looked at Field.

"Does the customer have anything to say?"

"Uh," Field was taken by surprise. "Sounds good."

"Customer service is our goal," Rudy sneered. "Be sure to fill out our online survey."

"Okay," Field said.

"Good Lord, Yadi," Rudy passed an exasperated laugh. "Where did you find..."

"He knows what's up," Yadi cut him off. "He's just playing along. Right, Field?"

"Right," Field nodded.

The car held little evidence that anyone else had owned it. Field found seventy-two cents in the change caddy between the driver and passenger seat, and a small pendant. The pendant had an inscription: "St. Christopher, patron of travelers, pray for us, protect us in our travels."

He was surprised Rudy, or someone in the impound lot, hadn't kept the change. He caught himself judging and didn't feel he had the room to do so. He was playing along, alright. Just like Yadi said, even though he was talking about getting Rudy's joke. He was playing along with something bigger.

But that room to judge seemed to expand with each mile he put behind him. The engine was so quiet. He was going to be able to visit a friend who was lonely thanks to this car, remind her how great she was until she didn't need reminding. All he did to earn this was glare at people who weren't living up to their end of a deal, and every so often keep them from harming his other friend.

"I'm helping people," he told himself.

He also told Lulu as part of the more detailed description of his job he provided when he came out to visit her for the first time since he discovered it was possible.

"You said that last time," she reminded him.

"Does it sound like we're not?"

"Do you really have to bully people if they don't pay on time?"

"We don't bully people."

"What did you call it last time?"

Field tried to think of what he called it last time, but couldn't before Lulu continued.

"Can't you do that thing where you take money out of their paycheck? That happened to my dad once."

"It's under the table, Lulu. I told you."

"You said Gonzo buys the appliances to sell them. Why doesn't he make it a real business?"

"He has. It has a name and everything. I'm not sure what it is. If he buys them with his own name, he can't sell them. It's against company policy or something."

Lulu sighed and surveyed the room as if making sure no one could hear them, but the coast was obviously clear. They sat in the coffee house at The Crossroads of The Valley where almost all of the customers used the drive-thru to caffeinate on their way to somewhere else. Field and Lulu had been the only people in the seating area since they walked in after her shift was over at the gift shop, aside from the baristas who worked behind the counter scurrying to help the motorists whose voices filled their headsets and whose faces appeared in the window.

"It sounds sleazy," she concluded her sigh. "Hiding his identity to conduct his business."

"I can always stick with punching the clock at the home store if it gets weird."

"If Gonzo will let you."

"What do you mean?"

"He holds such sway over you."

"Sway?"

"He controls you."

"Is this still about high school?"

"It started in junior high," she reminded him. "But no, it's not."

She stared out the window to see if her uncle had arrived yet to pick her up. Field shook his head slowly as though sifting through his thoughts for a new direction.

"I'm sorry," he said. "This isn't going the way I wanted it to."

"I'm sorry, too," she appeared to relax. "You're maybe the only person who can understand why things turned out the way they did. I should be nicer."

"Don't worry, Lulu. We're used to people not being nice to us."

Lulu smiled.

"I had this teacher," she said. "Excuse me. Professor. They call them professors in college."

"That would scare me."

"It's just a title. Anyway, this professor, she taught one of my education classes."

"Aren't all your classes about education?"

"The job of education. Learning to be an educator."

"Ah, I knew that," Field said with a grin that admitted he didn't.

"She talked about most people being 99 percent good, but there's a one percent that spills out every once in a while, and people like you and me, we're often the reason for that one percent. We take it more than most, because people get impatient with us, or they're afraid of us."

"Afraid of us?"

"Sure. They're afraid we take up too much attention and money, but they also feel bad for thinking that, since they're mostly good, so they get frustrated. And there we are."

"Coach used to tell us if it scares us, it's the right thing to do."

"Coach Gonzo?"

"No, the head coach. He was big on expressions. The assistants, like Gonzo, did most of the coaching."

"That's not a bad saying. But it needs context."

"I've heard that word before."

"It means, like, conditions. For example when you just used it now, it kind of doesn't work. I said that people are scared of us, so if doing the right thing is doing something that's scary, they should go ahead and be scared of us."

She looked out the window again for her uncle. It was a reasonable thing for her to do, but it bothered Field.

"Like I said," she continued, "you just have to consider the circumstances. If you're scared because you're thinking of being the first one to speak up about something bad that's happening, that's good fear to overcome."

He wondered if she was needling him again about his job, but decided it didn't matter. She made sense.

"I can't get over how great you sound," he said.

She smiled, but with some effort.

Field watched her sip her coffee.

"Sorry if I'm complimenting you too much," he offered.

"Sorry if I'm criticizing you too much."

He fell into a smile with her.

"You're not," he tried his best to sound convincing.

"It's good to see you doing so well. I was afraid they were going to use you, then toss you aside."

"I'm still an ex-high school star working at the local home store," he finally took a sip of his own. "Pretty lame. Like some country song."

"A country song would glorify it."

"Glorify," he swallowed. "I love the words you use."

"You've got a nice place of your own, and a car."

"I haven't really bought them. I've been given things, and I need to pay them off."

"Everyone does that."

"I've become normal," he toasted himself. "I finally made it."

"Miss Madeline would be proud. Do you ever see her?"

"She comes into the store. And it's Mrs. Berry, now that we're adults and she's not my counselor anymore."

"Not just Madeline?"

"Maybe if I saw her outside the store. She's really proud of you, that's for sure."

Lulu looked into her cup.

"Another reason to hide out here," she spoke into it.

"Come on. You're the first person on her case list who ever went to college."

"Maybe the next one will finish."

"Tell me more about your classes. It makes me feel smarter."

"It makes me feel dumber."

"Then tell me about your job. About the weird customers and about that artists that come in to sell their work."

She was happy to talk about other people for a while. It kept her from looking out the window.

Most of the sculptures were produced in bulk and arrived in boxes marked by return addresses from distant places. Some were unique. Some really were crafted by people Lulu had met.

One was a retired farmer who made money later in life selling his "secret recipe" livestock feed. Not a tremendous amount of money, because he didn't want to expand to a degree where he'd have to reveal his recipe in order to obtain the proper licenses and permits, but enough to allow him to sculpt rusty roosters from rakes and gear wheels.

Another was able to list "artist" as her profession. She was a graphic designer who worked from home, and spent time away from her computer by combing the valley for debris she could use for her abstract expressions. She lived in the coastal valley, in the town where Lulu and Field grew up, but found the inland terrain more filled with the discarded. She and Lulu spoke of various haunts in their hometown, and when Lulu mentioned her art exhibit from high school, the woman remembered it.

"Why didn't you stick with it?" the artist asked her.

"I only had one show in me," Lulu told her. "That was my one idea."

The artist praised her some more, recalled the faces of her classmates, how beautifully she captured the complexity underneath their otherwise blank expressions.

"Excuse me..."

Lulu interrupted her own story.

"I'm bragging."

"No you're not," Field encouraged her. "You're telling me what the artist told you."

"I'm trying to feel better about myself."

"Good," he smiled. "What else did she say?"

"What time is it?" Lulu avoided the question and looked out the window.

Field took out his phone.

"Is that a company phone?" she asked.

"Pretty much," he showed her the time. "I'm afraid to use it. All I do is answer it."

"I don't know why I asked for the time," she squinted at the screen. "He's done when the sun sets."

"So what else did the artist tell you?"

"That was the end of the story, Field."

"Should you have been an art major?"

"What?"

"Did she make you regret your decision?"

"I should go outside to make sure he can see me," she gathered her cup from the table and slid sideways on the chair.

"Just wondering," Field shrugged.

She stood and flashed a smirk.

Field asked about it.

"I was hoping you were kidding," she explained. "But you still don't do that."

"I joke around."

"I mean teasing. You don't have it in you. You're too sincere."

She downed her last sip and walked the cup to the trash bin.

"Ah," she finally saw what she was looking for through the window. "There he is."

She came over and kissed Field on the cheek.

"Can we do this again?" he asked.

"Of course."

"Is your schedule changing anytime soon?"

"Probably not. You can call the shop to be sure."

She trotted toward the door.

He waved goodbye with the phone.

"Keep it short if you do," she gestured to his prop. "Company phone."

He smiled and put it back in his pocket.

It rang as he lingered at The Crossroads in the sunset. He would have thought it was Lulu calling to taunt him if she had the number.

"We need you at the store," Gonzo said without a hello.

"I'll be there in about forty-five minutes."

"Where are you?"

"The valley."

"As in Business Valley?"

"Yes."

"Is there a meeting I forgot about? You're not taking initiative, are you? Don't do anything without running it by me or Yadi first."

"I was visiting an old friend."

"Oh. Well. Drive fast. I'll pay for your ticket if you get one."

Field was about to remind him of insurance costs, but the call was over.

He spent a moment enjoying how much more red and smoky the sun was on this horizon compared to the one at home, then lowered himself into his car and drove toward the perkier, yellow sun.

Its waning light was the only feature left by the time he reached the store. The lights in the parking lot had turned on, and as usual there were fewer cars in the hours before closing. Maybe more than usual, but hardly a freakish rush. He wondered what was so urgent. Perhaps some trucks were in back in need of unloading.

One of the elderly men who worked in the paint department approached him when he came in.

"Gonzo's up in the conference room."

Field nodded thanks and made his way across the floor and up the stairs. He opened the door and was ambushed by dozens of voices shouting "Surprise!"

His first instinct was to cover his ears and put his head down, but the sound subsided quickly enough and everyone was smiling so broadly that he managed to catch himself with some deep breaths. Gonzo emerged from the sea of noise and teeth with arms outstretched.

"Congratulations," he said. "Your name is going in the Ring of Honor at the high school."

"I thought that was for old people."

Everyone laughed, Gonzo loudest of all.

"Normally, they do like to wait a while," he explained. "But since you're about the most obvious candidate in school history, I convinced them to buck tradition and just do it."

"Did you say 'buck', Gonzo?" a voice shouted from the back of the room, "or something else?"

The laughter reignited. Gonzo continued.

"The ceremony will take place at the last home meet this season."

"Wow," Field started to recognize the faces of former teammates, and wrestlers who came before him who would come to the meets, including Yadi. Some of his more avid fans from around town were also there.

I was one of them.

We shared a brief hug once the party settled in, along with a perfunctory "How are you doing?" "Fine."

Gonzo pulled him aside soon after we had our exchange.

"We have a job tomorrow that would work a lot better with your car instead of Yadi's truck. You mind driving?"

"Not at all."

"That's my man."

He put an arm around Field and gestured across the room to Yadi with a grand thumb raising.

Yadi came over and play-wrestled Field into a hug before offering his congratulations. They arranged a time for Field to stop by and pick him up early the next morning.

I didn't notice anything out of the ordinary that evening. Field did seem more reserved than one might expect at receiving such an honor. He accepted people's handshakes and hugs as though receiving condolences at a funeral for a troubled family member about whom people aren't sure what to say. I assumed he was overwhelmed, which was true enough, but I'm afraid I use that as an excuse.

After rehashing highlights from the party the night before, he and Yadi fell silent for most of the drive.

"See this road?" Yadi pointed ahead of them as they sped upward toward the range of hills where the abandoned ranger station stood.

He kept his finger fixed on an opening along a barbed wire fence that led to a single-lane dirt road.

"We're going to turn in there on the way back. It leads to that big old tower."

"Okay."

Field drove another quarter-mile before asking "What for?"

Yadi exhaled for about as long as Field imagined he could.

"You'll see," is all he said when he ran out of air.

As he directed Field where to exit and which streets to take, Field realized where they were headed. He hoped their destination was merely in the vicinity of the area he was thinking about, not the specific place.

Even when they pulled up to the beaten-down converted motel, he held out hope that their job involved one of the other units, not the one in the middle of the second story with the scared woman inside.

"Keep going," Yadi instructed him.

Field relaxed.

"Drive around back," Yadi continued.

Field tensed up again.

They parked along the street that led to the half-vacant shopping center with the grocery store in its midsection.

"Now what?" Field dared to ask after he turned off the engine.

"We wait," Yadi slouched in the passenger seat and put a foot on the dashboard.

"For what?"

"More like who."

"That woman?"

"Yup. A buddy of mine cut the power to her apartment last night. She's got some spoiled food she needs to replace. She'll be heading to the store when it opens."

"The store is probably open already."

"She won't go to the big franchise. She'll go to the little carniceria with the hand-painted sign that opens at ten."

When she appeared at the end of the block pushing her upright shopping cart, Field checked the time and confirmed Yadi's assumption, which took his mind off what might happen next.

Until Yadi saw her, too.

"Put a hand over your face, or look sideways. I don't want her to recognize you."

Field complied.

Yadi bent over so she wouldn't see him at all. He turned his head toward the window facing the sidewalk. When she passed by, he sprang from the car, grabbed her, and dove into the backseat. He was too fast and she was too shocked to make any noise beyond a confused grunt.

"Let's go," he ordered.

Field started the engine.

"Where?" he looked in the rearview mirror and couldn't see them.

"I told you on the way."

"Oh. Yeah."

Field looked higher in the mirror to see down low.

Yadi finished stuffing a sock in her mouth, then pulled twine from his jacket pocket and started to tie her hands together.

"Now!" he snarled.

Field pulled away from the curb. He looked straight into the mirror to see if anyone was behind them. Her shopping cart stood alone on the sidewalk, shrinking into the center of the frame.

Yadi stayed out of sight after finishing his work, leaning over onto the woman to prevent her from sitting up. He whispered to her in Spanish, as though trying to put a child to bed. Field stole occasional glances at them and tried to make sure his own eyes were not as wide as hers.

When they were on the highway, drawing closer to the hilly border, Yadi gave him further orders.

"Create some space behind you before we get to the turn. Let people pass."

Field nodded rather than saying "okay," as he wasn't sure he could utter a word without his voice cracking.

"When we get there, pull over onto the shoulder if there's any cars coming from the opposite direction and wait until everything is clear before making the left."

Field mustered a hum to go with his nod.

He didn't need to follow orders when it came time to make the turn. No one was visible in either direction. He slowed into the swerve and kept his speed down as the asphalt gave way to dirt. The opening in the barbed wire was just wide enough to pass through.

"There used to be a gate," Yadi narrated from the rear. "Someone unhinged it, and nobody bothered to replace it."

Field focused on the road as it climbed and curved. His tires spun whenever they hit a patch of loose earth, spraying gravel into the wheel well and along the bottom of the chassis. The distance to the abandoned station was lengthened by the treacherous cut of the path.

They wound around three hills before rising to the top of the one with the tower perched on it.

"Don't park next to it. Stop here."

Field obeyed.

"We don't want the car to catch a reflection from the sun and be seen from the highway," Yadi justified his command.

He climbed out of the back and towed the woman toward the station.

Age and neglect were a lot more apparent on the building now that they were close to it. The corrugated metal was rusted along the edges, and around the perforations where it had torn. The whole structure appeared to be buckling.

"You too, Field," Yadi called him out.

Field lurched out of the driver's seat and followed them.

What could be heard of the woman's muffled cries seemed to escape through the rest of her body. Yadi kicked open a door at the base of the tower and once they were all inside, her sobs echoed louder.

The ceilings were high, including the roof that fanned out from the tower, and the walls were thin. Beams of sunlight pierced the seams in the metal. The remains of some steel steps and platforms led up the gullet of the tower. Yadi grabbed an aluminum chair from a row of them lined up along the wall by the door and dragged it with one hand as he tugged the woman with the other. The chair legs screeched across the cement floor and drowned what they could hear of the woman. He lugged them both to the far end of the building, heading for a stairway that led to nowhere, as the platform it used to connect with had collapsed.

When the noise stopped with the chair, Yadi gestured for Field to catch up.

"Tie her to the post," he dangled some more twine. "I'll do her feet. It's easy to get kicked if you don't know what you're doing. I'll show you when you're done."

Field wrapped the twine around her as many times as the length allowed. He avoided looking at her. When he was finished, he watched and listened as Yadi instructed him on how to tie feet to the legs of a chair without getting kicked in the face.

After Yadi said, "And that's that," he straightened up and walked toward the door.

"We're not staying?" Field followed him.

"This is a delivery. Our job is done."

"Who's picking her up?"

"Nobody you want to meet. And they want to remain anonymous, so it works out for everyone."

Field looked back at the woman before they walked out the door. Each of her eyes were as big as the sock frothing from her mouth.

He closed the door.

The echoes of the room were replaced with the wind whispering through the hills.

"Wait," Field asked, processing the abrupt shift, as though they had changed a channel.

"What?" Yadi stopped and turned to face him.

"Why don't we just take the refrigerator, or whatever they bought?"

Yadi laughed, and for the first time sounded like one of the kids who used to make fun of him, rather than a friend.

"You still think this is about appliances?" he asked in a tone that paired well with his laugh.

Field didn't bother answering.

Yadi took a deep breath and looked away.

"We did take what they bought," he said.

Field tried to put everything together.

"Don't ask me anymore questions," Yadi said. "I don't know how much Gonzo wants you to know."

He started walking again.

"Yadi…"

"Talk to Gonzo!"

Field navigated the dirt road back to the highway. He couldn't think of anything to say that didn't involve questions about what they had done.

"Take a right," Yadi said when the highway loomed ahead. "We have some more business in the valley. Normal business."

Field did his job well the rest of the day. He never looked meaner. If he looked scary enough, maybe the customers wouldn't miss any payments, and wouldn't be sent to the tower.

He stayed silent until on their way home, when they passed by the entrance to the dirt road.

"What are they going to do to her?"

"I told you not to ask any questions."

"I haven't said anything for hours."

Yadi sighed.

"Try not to think about it."

"Are they going to kill her?"

"Would you rather we do it ourselves?"

Field concentrated on the road ahead as it slid out of the hills, sloping toward the pastures of grass that were golden because they were dead. The gold spread across each side of the highway. Cows grazed in it. Farms in the distance formed patches of green attached to tree lines that obscured the houses and barns behind them. He didn't know what else to do to take his mind away from the woman's eyes and the visceral noises shaking through her body.

When they planed onto the flatlands, a flash of light bounced off the rearview mirror and forced him to squint. He adjusted it and noticed the source. A reflection was coming from the base of the abandoned station. Someone was parked there.

Tears soaked his eyelashes, which brushed his sunglasses and fogged the lenses.

In case Yadi noticed, he was prepared to blame the light shining in his eyes, which was true in a sense.

Yadi didn't seem to notice, though, until Field dropped him off.

"Talk to Gonzo," he gently reminded him.

He didn't need to be reminded. He knew he had to talk to him. The problem was that he had to look at him first, and Field wasn't sure he could.

# CHAPTER SEVEN: CONSEQUENCES

Field wanted to talk to Lulu as much as he wanted to avoid Gonzo, but didn't want to involve her, so he stayed away from everyone for as long as he could.

Gonzo should have been more difficult to dodge, but he offered Field a conspicuous break from their trips to Business Valley without actually contacting him. Field would clock in for his shifts at the store, expecting Gonzo to call him into his office or Yadi to show up, but he wouldn't hear from either of them.

He went to a wrestling meet for the first time since his charitable graduation from high school, thinking perhaps it would provide a distraction, but all the people approaching him and telling him how great he was triggered a nauseous churn of self-hatred.

During the initial phase of his exile, he wouldn't look up at the window of Gonzo's office, as the old coach often stood behind the glass surveying the floor. Weeks into his isolation, he started to glance upward on occasion, but did not see him. It started to feel like a game of hide-and-seek in which Field had found such a great hiding place that everyone stopped looking for him. Eeriness overcame him and he spent longer spells looking up at the window. He didn't want to call Gonzo, or Yadi, but he wanted answers.

"Miss me?"

A hand clamped down on his shoulder as he stared upward.

He jumped and found Gonzo grinning at him, shifting his hand clamp into a shoulder pat.

He didn't know how to respond.

Gonzo didn't wait.

"Let's go to lunch," he stopped patting his shoulder and steered it. "Our old favorite, where we used to go after wrestling practice. I'll drive."

"I'll see you there."

Gonzo flashed anger then breathed back into the pleasant.

"See you there," he agreed.

Field tried to map out a line of questioning on his way to the rickety tacqueria. He couldn't fool himself into thinking he would be able to guide the conversation, so he settled on a few points he wanted to make regardless of where the coach was taking things.

It was later in the afternoon, past the lunch rush, so the line was sparse. Gonzo was a couple of customers away from the counter. Field joined him without saying anything.

"You used to be so hungry when we came here," Gonzo reminisced.

Field nodded.

"Can you still handle the usual? Now that you're not training?"

"Probably not. Too much food."

"That's what I thought," Gonzo chuckled. "Which part of the order do you want? My treat."

"No."

"Excuse me?"

"I don't want your money."

Gonzo glanced up and down the line before humbling himself.

"I understand. But let me explain, and let me buy you lunch while I explain."

Field exhaled.

"Fine."

He left his order with Gonzo and grabbed a pair of rolled-up napkins with silverware wrapped inside them from the pile on the counter. He found a table surrounded by other empty tables. He spent his minutes alone trying to remember what he wanted to say and resigning himself to probably forgetting them once the conversation started.

"I know you still like water," Gonzo said as he brought their two cups to the table. "Staying away from soda might be the most important thing you learned from wrestling."

Field was deciding which question to lead with when Gonzo struck first.

"I'm sorry about what happened," he said. "I was hoping you would never have to deal with that kind of situation, which was foolish of me. It's been a couple of years since we had to go that far. Yadi went through the same thing you are now, and I hated to see it, so I guess I wanted to believe our clients had learned their lesson. Maybe they did, but eventually we get enough new customers, and they've only heard rumors."

"So you're a coyote."

Gonzo laughed as he unrolled his utensils.

"I don't think anyone has ever said that to my face. I like it better than 'human trafficker'. That's disrespectful to the clients. Makes them sound like cars, like machines. They're people, searching for a better life."

"That lady's life didn't look so great even before you killed her."

"Me?" the coach arched his eyebrows. "Don't you mean 'we'?"

Field looked down at the table and shielded his eyes from Gonzo, which didn't prevent his tears from splashing onto the table, and Gonzo from seeing them.

"Our order should be up soon," the coach said. "I'll go wait for it."

Field spent the duration of their time apart settling himself down, unable to consider his next move.

Gonzo returned with their order and ate quietly while Field stayed behind his hands resting on his forehead.

"None of this would have happened if the customers had been responsible," Gonzo tried to soothe him. "It's not your fault."

More tears dropped onto the table from behind his shield.

"We run a family business," Gonzo continued, eating heartily. "My cousin handles things on the southern end. He recruits, screens, and helps set up the payment plans. We've worked in the same town for years. They know us. We really do hook them up with appliances, sometimes a place to rent, so when they pay us it launders the money at the same time, at least some of it. We're a trusted name. But that trust works both ways. If you think that woman's life was bad in the valley, you should have seen it before. And how does she and her husband choose to repay us? By not paying us."

"Who are the killers that pick them up at the old ranger station?" Field wasn't ready to look up.

"They're like a collection agency. We have all the same things big businesses do, only we don't bury them under misleading names."

Field finally rose from behind his cover.

"Why can't you just send them back to your cousin?"

"Getting them out is just as expensive as getting them in, Field, and they haven't paid us in full for either direction. It's not a charity."

"Turn them in," Field started to feel stronger. "Call la migra with an anonymous tip or something. Let them handle it."

"Some of our other clients could be swept up in the process. Besides, they might rat us out. Our customers are too scared to go to the police. But bring the police to them? They might talk."

Whatever strength Field had gained was sapped. He slumped and stared at his food, but the kind of strength he needed didn't come from food.

"You aren't thinking of talking, are you, Field?"

"No," Field emphasized. "I just want out."

"Okay," Gonzo shrugged. "But where will you go?"

"I'll work at the store. You could keep an eye on me that way. I'll go back to normal."

"I mean where will you go when you can't pay for anything anymore?"

"I'll work more hours."

"You were doing that already, Field. Nobody worked more than you, and it still wasn't enough to pay for that shitty old place you were about to be evicted from, and the repairs on that shitty old car that was about to break down. There aren't enough hours on the floor to make a difference."

"I'd get another job."

"I hope you're not thinking of moving back home."

"What do you care? As long as I don't narc."

Gonzo smiled at him.

Field avoided eye contact by unraveling his silverware and starting to eat.

"Your mother once told me a funny story," Gonzo said. "Maybe she told you already. Have you heard the one about how you got your name?"

"It's because we live in farm country."

"That's what I thought, too. I figured someday I would use it to pitch the family business to you. 'It's destiny,' I would say. 'You were meant to help put people in the fields.' But then one night after you went to bed and I finished spackling a wall one of your idiot brothers had kicked in, your mother was a little more drunk than usual. She started talking about the day you were born, and how she still wasn't sure what to call you right up until she had to fill in the birth certificate. She filled out the rest of the form, and the name was blank. The nurse told her to write in the name field. Your mother took the nurse literally and wrote in the name, Field. The nurse saw it and said, 'No, the name field is the space where you write in the name of your baby. Call him whatever you want.' Your mother could have laughed it off, blamed it on being loopy after giving birth, but she stuck with it because she didn't want to admit she made a mistake. She laughed about it when she told me. A loud, drunk, stupid laugh. Your name is a joke to her."

Field stopped eating, but stayed focused on the plate.

"If you don't believe me, ask her," Gonzo said.

Field kept his attention on the morass of cheese and beans.

"Oh..." Gonzo elongated the word in mock recollection. "That's right. You're not speaking to her. A wise choice, by the way. Your family won't stand for any of its members succeeding, not as long as they're still losers. And you know how long that's gonna be? Forever."

Field started to eat again as though Gonzo wasn't there.

"I want to build you up, Field, not tear you down. If you can find somebody else who feels the same way, and has the means to make it happen, by all means, run with them. In the meantime, let me know when you're ready to get back to changing lives."

He stood up and took some cash from his wallet, running his hand along the bills as though trying to elongate them before putting the display on top of what was left of Field's teardrops.

"You never got paid for the station run," he captioned the exhibition.

Field wasn't sure he could swallow the food he had in his mouth.

"Take the rest of the day off," Gonzo said on his way out. "See you around the store."

Field forced down his last bite.

He contemplated the short stack of hundreds, hoping maybe someone would come and take it away. If he left without it, someone would probably chase him down and give it back. He didn't want anyone else to be touched by Gonzo's business.

A spoon sat on the table, the one utensil he had not used from the set inside the napkin. He picked it up. It felt cold to the touch. He brushed it lightly along his temple, and down his cheek. He continued to run the spoon around his face until it put him in a trance.

When an employee asked him if everything was all right, her voice startled him. He then noticed how apprehensive she was, as if she had lost a bet over who was going to check on the freak rubbing his face with a spoon.

He told her he was fine. He was able to respond because the answer was easy, because it wasn't true, but what was expected. Any kind of speaking that involved forming thoughts was not possible. There were only questions from customers and answers from employees. People were off-limits. He wondered how long this would last.

He wasn't sure he wanted the rest of the day off. It felt like being dumped by the side of the road. He extended the metaphor, imagining if there was anybody he would most want to pick him up, and he could only think of one person.

It was still early. Even the lengthy drive would put him at The Crossroads hours before her shift ended, if she was working. He decided not to call ahead and check. A far-flung, isolated drive sounded soothing. Discovering Lulu at the end of it would be a bonus. He swept the money into his pocket and launched.

He tried not to stare at the haunted station as it towered over the transition from one valley to the next. It hovered in his peripheral vision, the area the eye can't see but the brain fills in with what it assumes is there. His brain constructed a shiny blur floating above the hills, a light daring him not to look.

He saw Lulu before she saw him.

She was straightening up some thin sweatshirts bearing the logo of the nearest university, which was fifty miles away from The Crossroads. She appeared lost in her work, so he approached slowly.

When she glanced up and saw him, he recoiled with an apologetic grin and wave. She looked upset, but then walked briskly up to him and clutched him in the kind of hug that used to get them in trouble in elementary school.

"Where have you been?" she demanded in a whisper.

"They needed me at the store a lot."

"I really wanted to see you."

She started to rock him back and forth, roughly half his size, controlling the motion.

"You did?"

He was delirious with feeling friendship again.

"I'm sorry for jumping you like this," she said into his chest.

"Don't be," he barely managed to say.

"I've been dumping all my emotions on my poor co-workers, and they need a break."

"Okay," he assured her, but confusion started to seep into his embrace.

"Plus it's not the same with them."

"Did something happen?"

"My aunt disappeared."

He halted the rocking, but kept her head buried in his arms so she couldn't see his face.

"My uncle is so sad," she continued into his shoulder. "He can barely move."

"When did she disappear?"

"A few weeks ago."

"What do they think happened?"

"There is no 'they'. She was undocumented, so there's no investigation. It's like she was never here."

"I'm so very, very sorry, Lulu."

He had never delivered a more earnest apology in his life.

"My uncle is convinced she's dead."

"Why does he think that?" he tightened his grip on her for a moment before realizing what he was doing. He overcorrected and let her go.

"He won't say much to me," she looked down at the floor more than him, as though she was also concerned with giving anything away. "He mumbles about being involved in some bad things. He blames himself. Dad came over to console him. He told him not give up hope, but then they started talking really softly so I couldn't hear, and Dad got upset. He asked why he didn't come to them for help, and they argued, so my family has been keeping their distance."

Field couldn't help but feel relieved to hear her say that. He sighed, and played it off as distress.

"He hasn't worked since it happened," she elaborated. "He lays on the couch all day and night. He's practically paralyzed."

The relief was squeezed by guilt.

"Any chance you can give me a ride home from work?" she asked.

Field was taken by surprise.

"I totally understand if you can't," she followed up. "But I've been hitching rides with my co-workers, and I'd love to leave them alone."

"Sure," he answered.

He was afraid he sounded bewildered.

"Of course," he compensated in the most assuring tone he could summon.

"Thank you!" Lulu rushed another hug. "I'm not off for another couple of hours. But you probably have work to do, and I'll wait for you if I have to."

"Actually I have the rest of the day off."

"Oh no," she covered her mouth. "I'm sorry. You don't have to spend it waiting for me. Never mind."

"It's okay. I want to."

"Are you sure?"

"I've killed time before at The Crossroads. I can kill some more."

She groaned gratefully, kissed him on the cheek, thanked him, and said "See you at five" as she walked away down the aisle.

Field started at the barbeque place.

He wasn't hungry, but liked the view from the deck that wrapped around the back looking out across the valley floor. He ordered a fountain drink and filled it with water, chalking up the money as his lease on the seat he was taking up. The valley floor was a patchwork of green, brown, and yellow based on whether each patch of land was producing, tilled, or fallow. He wondered how to calculate the odds of Lulu being related to that one client. They dealt with a small subset of the valley's workforce, so maybe the coincidence was not as remarkable as it was unfortunate.

The eastbound highway ran alongside the canal that brought water from the mountains in the distance. He watched the line of asphalt and the line of water disappear into the haze of the horizon and thought of how large those projects were. He would have liked to live in a time when people built things like highways, dams, canals, and bridges. The things people built in his generation to make life flow were hard to see, riding on invisible waves between electronic devices, understood by people who didn't need the kind of skills Field had to offer. He wished he could be a part of something so big and important that helped make people's lives better. Gonzo told him he was, but it wasn't true. His world was small and mean. The only big things about it were the holes it made in people's lives.

He went back inside to refill his cup and saw Yadi's friend manning the smoker behind the glass by the kitchen. He noticed Field and smiled. Field smiled back, but not very well, as it occurred to him he might run into Yadi. He threw away his cup and exited.

Once on the wood-slat sidewalk out front, he turned in a direction he had never been, toward the edge, rather than toward the gift shop and coffee house.

When he reached the end, where the wood planks gave way to cement, he noticed a path that led to the rear of the buildings. He followed it and proceeded down the weedy grade to the canal. A chain link fence prevented access to the paved shore. He leaned against the wires and watched the water flow. Some great white egrets stood upstream. They were stalking creatures in the grass above the lip of the canal. Even if there were fish in the manufactured stream, it would be hard for the egrets to stand on the sloped sides that slid into water that was too deep for them to forage and spear their prey. But they found a way to use the water for hunting. They adapted.

He may have made eye contact with one of the egrets. The bird appeared to be looking his way, but the eye facing him was unblinking and seemed capable of looking everywhere at once. It speared a frog and gulped it down in a series of shudders and headshakes. After it swallowed the frog, the egret paused, as though letting some indigestion pass. Once satisfied that everything went through, its first move was to take flight. It unfurled a pair of white angel wings and lifted off, its long legs dangling like wind chimes until it started to move forward and tuck in its legs as a plane would its landing gear.

Field followed its rise. As his eyes gravitated back to earth, he spotted some people on the barbeque balcony looking at him. He felt shifty and shuffled back up the hill to the center, deciding on the coffee house as the most discreet place to wait.

He positioned himself by a window where he could see the vehicles picking up their drinks at the drive-thru window. He checked the license plates to see how many were from other states. He listened to the conversations of those who came inside to order and could tell when they were from someplace else, as their talk revolved around where they had been and how much longer until they reached where they were going. Field wondered how far he would have to go for a fresh start. Even more of an issue is what he would do when he arrived at his blank slate, how he would afford to draw on it and color it in.

Lulu found him looking out his window and thanked him for waiting.

He asked her if she wanted anything.

"I'd love to hang out, but I don't want to keep my uncle waiting."

Field understood.

As they drove out of the parking lot, he knew where they were going.

"How did you know to turn right?" she asked.

"Oh," he stalled. "That's where most people live, isn't it?"

"I guess so. Or you had too much coffee and it scrambled your brain."

"You need to give me directions the rest of the way."

He listened and followed her lead. She took them on a different route than he would have chosen. When they arrived at the scene of the crime, Field was afraid his shirt was jumping, his heartbeat visible. Maybe she knew. He had established a reputation. How many giant gringos could there be traveling around the valley menacing people?

"Do you want to come in?" she asked him as they idled behind the row of cars facing the bottom floor.

"No," he stared up at the door. "I'd better not."

It was only a door, but walking through it had changed everything. It seemed to look down on him, even taunt him.

"Tio won't mind," she assured him.

"Is that his name?"

"Oh, come on. 'Tio' means uncle. You know that."

"Of course. Sorry. I'm tired."

"All that sitting around waiting for me."

"Lulu..."

"I know, you don't have to tell me it's okay again. I'm just thankful and a little embarrassed."

She kissed him on the cheek.

"Maybe next time?" she asked.

"Sure. Next time."

"I'm holding you to that," she smiled as she slid out of the passenger seat.

Field smiled back, but hung his head as soon as she stood up.

Looking down at his lap reminded him of the money in his pocket that Gonzo had given him at lunch.

"Lulu!" he cut the engine and jumped out of the car.

"You're coming up after all?"

"No," he caught up to her and was about to dig for the cash, then thought better of brandishing that much money in front of all those units.

"Come here," he gestured for her to follow him into the tunnel where the ice machine and vending machines probably used to be when it was a motel.

"What?" she held on to her smile in the face of curiosity.

"The reason they need me at the store so much is they made me a manager."

"Okay. Congratulations."

"They paid me a bonus when I took the job."

He took out the cash and handed it to her.

"Please take it."

"Field..." she studied the money.

"You said your uncle hasn't been working. Maybe this will help."

"Oh, it will definitely help."

"Good."

"But..."

"No!" he said too forcefully.

Lulu acted more startled than she actually was.

"No," he quieted down. "No buts. I need you to take it."

"You do?"

"I don't have anyone," Field came up with an excuse that was grounded in truth.

He had never lied so much in his life, and needed to make his story as real as possible to have any chance at getting away with it.

"I'm making all this money," he continued. "I have the condo, the car, all the stuff we're supposed to have. But I want to do something good with it, too."

Lulu looked down at the money, then back up at Field.

"Well..." she took a long drag on the word. "If it makes you feel better."

"Thank you," he hugged her.

"You're welcome?" she emphasized the question mark.

"There's more," Field realized as he separated from her.

Lulu reverted back to hesitancy.

"Until he gets back on his feet," he added.

She reconsidered.

"That could motivate him, actually," she pondered aloud. "He'll want to pay you back."

"No, no. That's how we got in this mess in the first place."

Lulu fell from her thoughts into confusion.

"Isn't it?" Field tried to cover his tracks.

"I'm not sure what you mean."

"You said he told you he was involved in some bad things. I don't want him to do anything like that to pay me back."

"No need to get ahead of ourselves," she dismissed his concern. "Let him pay you like five bucks a month if it comes to that. At the very least he'll want to get back on his feet and stop accepting your charity."

He wanted to correct her.

It wasn't charity, but he couldn't think of the right word.

Reparations, maybe.

Or amends.

Restitution.

Not that he could have used any of those words. To do so would be to confess.

"Any way I can help," he assured her.

They embraced and then walked out of the tunnel.

Lulu took the stairs up to the second floor and disappeared behind that door with a wave.

Field drove back to the home store.

He strode into Gonzo's office and told him he wanted to make as much money as he possibly could without collapsing from exhaustion. He suggested that he and Yadi go solo whenever plausible to double their efforts.

Gonzo had to remind him that traveling in pairs was about safety, about having each other's backs.

"Like the spotters for the mascots at Disneyland," Field commented.

"Did you hear that comparison from Yadi?" Gonzo smiled.

"Did he get it from you?"

Gonzo bowed his head, delighted to see his wishes come true.

"What changed your mind?" he asked.

Field was resigned to make the best of an awful situation. He thought Gonzo may ask him that, so he had prepared his lies this time.

"It's tough out there," he said, which was true enough, and the reason he decided to use it. "I'm lucky to have a chance. Or, I guess 'opportunity' is the word people like to use."

"My favorite word."

Field thought it was one of those words that was easy to hide behind.

They worked out a schedule that barely put Field in the store. He was in Business Valley practically every day.

"Making up for lost time," Gonzo said more than once.

Yadi was glad to have him back.

"I thought maybe we lost you," he said.

"I felt lost," Field played with the word as they traveled between clients one day.

"I was talking business," Yadi appeared to clutch the steering wheel tighter.

"I know."

"But if you want to talk about what happened."

"No. I don't."

"Thank God," Yadi exhaled and loosened his grip.

Field laughed, as much as he didn't want to.

They emerged from the small town that was bisected by the highway and faced an open stretch of road.

"Did you ever take Psychology with Mrs. Nava in high school?" Yadi asked.

"Psychology wasn't on my IEP."

"There's this theory, I'm not sure what it's called. I remembered it after my first run to the station."

"Who made that run with you?"

"Gonzo."

"Really?"

"He was still in the field then. Not much, but he came out for the big jobs. He tried to make me feel better about that first delivery, but it didn't work. Did he try with you?"

"I didn't give him much of a chance," Field caught a glimpse of a 'No Hunting' sign stuck to a fencepost along the barbed wire boundary that bordered a fallow field. "I avoided him."

"Glad I wasn't the only one you avoided."

"Sorry. So the psychology thing helped?"

"A little, I guess. It explained some things. The idea is that the farther away you are from some bad thing, the easier it is to do. They ask people about this train heading down a track toward a bunch of people, and if they'd pull a lever to shift the train onto a track that will kill one person instead of the whole bunch. Pretty much everyone says sure, they'll do that. Sacrifice one to save many. But if they have to push someone onto the track to save all those people, they won't do it."

"One person could stop a train?"

"It's more like a cable car. The point is, they'll pull a lever but they won't push a person."

Field thought it over for a quarter mile.

"Who are we saving?" he asked.

"What do you mean?"

"When we bring someone to the abandoned station, we're pulling a lever instead of pushing a person. I get that. But who are the people we're supposed to be saving?"

Yadi swept his arm across the country ahead of them.

"The ones who deserve to be here," he proclaimed. "The ones who keep their word."

Field quieted down again.

Yadi slowed down as they approached a dirt road that led to an outcropping of houses that looked deserted if not for the vehicles parked around them.

"Let's see that mean mug," Yadi chatted him up as their tires crackled toward the decrepit collection.

Field stared blankly at him.

"Still got it," Yadi grinned.

They settled next to a house with its garage open. Piles of discarded auto parts seemed to be lit by the reflection of a shining new water heater in the corner.

"I know you want to start taking some leads," Yadi said while he set the brake. "Pero no habla ingles aqui. Hang back on this one."

Field nodded and followed him.

A woman entered the garage from a side door. She was already crying. Field halted while Yadi proceeded to greet her in the middle of the garage's opening, making it look like the two of them were on a stage. Yadi comforted her while she spoke through her tears. He patted her shoulder when it was his turn to deliver his lines, and gave her one more hug before rejoining Field in the audience.

"What's going on?" Field asked as they climbed back into Yadi's truck.

"Her husband got busted running an errand for the money men."

"The money men?"

"The guys in charge."

"In charge of what?"

"Us."

Yadi started the engine while Field considered what that might mean.

"I take it Gonzo didn't tell you he has a boss, too," Yadi said as he gently waved goodbye to the woman.

"No. He didn't."

"Well..." Yadi concentrated on making a three-point turn and maneuvering his truck back to the highway. "...I'm not sure it's my place to tell you, but the Diaz family kind of forced my hand here. Gonzo will have to let it out eventually. When he does, act surprised."

Field waited for the rest of the story, which Yadi picked up once they were back on the highway at cruising speed.

"It was just border crossings for a long time. Gonzo and his cousin were doing well. Not all that fat, but a pretty sweet side hustle. The big crime family out here made him an offer to expand. The money was too tempting, or maybe they didn't give him much choice. Either way, Gonzo took it. Since then, they use our customers as free labor. It's supposed to help them pay off their debts, but they don't get much of a cut. Gonzo keeps most of it."

"What do they have them do?"

"The wholesale side of their business. Things they don't want to expose their people to. Running drugs or weapons. A lot of 'drive this car to Los Mochis and don't look in the trunk' kind of stuff. That's what Soledad's husband back there got popped for. I heard our guys even deliver car bombs sometimes. But I think they just tell them that so nobody looks in the trunk. The family takes care of the retail side."

"Who are they? This family?"

"I'm not sure anymore. They change hands all the time. Like a bank."

Yadi started to giggle. Field assumed he was enjoying his bank analogy.

"There's also some prostitution," Yadi said.

Field glared at him.

"I'm not laughing at that," he explained. "Prostitution isn't funny. Though it sounds kind of funny to say it isn't funny."

Field waited for his answer.

"All right, hard ass," Yadi smirked. "The prostitution bothered Gonzo, too, so he tried to get around it by only recruiting men for the crossings. Like there's no Spanish word for 'gay'. But Gonzo is too much of a dumb macho fuck to see anything he doesn't want to see. And it was too late to start drawing lines in the sand, anyway. There was only one he shouldn't have crossed."

Field watched an almond orchard pass by. He caught a glimpse of some workers down one of the rows. They were hard to see amongst the trunks of the trees and the low-hanging branches, and he would not have noticed them if he hadn't been looking their way.

"The money is that much better?" Field wanted his question to sound like a statement.

"You know those buildings I own?"

"Sure."

"Gonzo gave me the cash. They're in my name to clean the money. That's why we stop at the casino and cash in those chips. It's why we charge two thousand dollars for a beat-up washing machine."

Field continued to look out the window.

"I didn't know there was a drug problem here," he said.

"Here is full of shitty work that's hard to come by and people with no sense of place," Yadi snickered. "Why wouldn't there be a drug problem?"

Field kept his attention on a scattered herd of cattle grazing on what was left of the brittle grass that had been baked over the summer.

"It's not like drinking," Yadi took the edge off his tone. "People don't do it out in the open."

The herd passed. Open fields filled the window.

"You're gonna see some of it today, though."

Field wondered what he meant, but didn't want to ask any more questions. He felt stupid for not understanding the work he was involved in, like he used to feel in school.

When they reached the last town they had driven through on their way out to the Diaz garage, Yadi slowed onto a street that funneled into its two-block business district, which could have been described as looking sleepy if the buildings were quaint, but instead looked dazed. From the punched-out and exhausted downtown they veered onto a side road that drew them into a residential area with rows of houses that still offered hope in the bright colors residents had painted the trim around the door and window frames, aqua blues and lime greens to accent the drab tans and grays that had come standard in the tract.

Except for the house they pulled up to, which may as well have been planted by the dusty fields in the weary circle of homes that included the Diaz garage. It could have been used by the Rotary Club for their annual Haunted House fundraiser.

Yadi pulled into its driveway and walked through the front door as if he lived there. Field jogged to catch up, then froze in the doorway. The smell would have had him retching if the visuals had not been so arresting. The odor of human waste was overwhelmed by the sight of people slumped along the base boards. They were indistinguishable gaunt figures, neither women nor men, looking as though they had been slammed against the walls as part of a relentless beating before sliding down into variations of the fetal position. Field wondered if they would bother to get up if the house caught on fire. The only movement he noticed was the occasional pipe being raised and lit.

Yadi was bending over and looking closely at each one as he passed them by.

"Not in the family room," he captioned his search as he stood up straight and glanced around to make sure he didn't miss anyone.

Field followed him down the hall into what was supposed to be a bedroom, which was lined with about as many bodies in roughly half the space. Yadi dug up what he was looking for within a few inspections.

"Tony?" he said to a face with its eyes closed. "Is that you?"

The body responded to the name. The eyes opened.

"Hmm," Tony recognized Yadi but had to shake his voice back to life. "What's up, Yadi?"

"I almost didn't recognize you," Yadi took a knee in front of him now that he had confirmation. "Have you lost weight?"

Tony tried to answer, but his voice still needed to stretch.

"I'm kidding, Tony. I mean, you have lost weight, but nobody wants your secret."

Tony chuckled.

"So how high are you?" Yadi asked. "Are you going to remember this conversation?"

"I'm good."

"Define good."

"I ran out of money last night. I'm just crashing now."

"Crashing as in going through withdrawals, or sleeping?"

"What the fuck do you want, Yadi?"

"Ah, signs of life. Good. Let's talk."

Yadi gestured for Field to come closer.

Tony's eyes widened.

"Is that G.G.?"

Yadi put his head down and stifled a smile.

"G.G.?" Field asked.

"Gringo Grande," Yadi elaborated.

"You're real," Tony smiled and coughed a weary laugh.

"Disappearing for a while only added to your legend," Yadi replied to Field's baffled gawk.

"Is this it, then?" Tony's smile gave way to glassy-eyed dread. "Have you come for me?"

"Not like that," Yadi assured him. "You've got time. But Field here, G.G., is in charge of your case."

Field looked even more quizzically at Yadi.

"You wanted to do some independent work," Yadi shrugged at him. "Tony speaks English."

"What case?" Tony found some energy. "Didn't you hear?"

"Yes," Yadi turned his attention back to Tony. "And we're very sorry to hear about your father. He's a good man."

"Are they going after him in jail?"

"No. The people on the top floor understand the costs of doing business. People get busted sometimes, like your papi. Product is seized. Which reminds me, you didn't seize any of the product for yourself before the run, did you?"

"Never saw the car," Tony rolled the back of his head along the wall. "They picked him up and brought him wherever it was parked."

"See? Smart people in upper management. You don't get that high by being an idiot."

Tony started to chuckle.

"What?" Yadi wanted in on the joke.

"I get high because I'm an idiot."

"Ahhh," Yadi pointed playfully at him. "Not bad, Tony. Not bad. Three days in a crack house and you still got it. Which goes to show, you're not really an idiot, are you?"

Tony didn't answer.

"Tony?"

"No."

"No what?"

"I'm not an idiot."

"You're gonna do some good work," Yadi patted him on the shoulder. "It's kind of refreshing to think of our job as changing lives for the better. Isn't it, Field?"

"What kind of work?" Tony asked before Field could respond.

Yadi exhaled and prepared his explanation.

"The men upstairs aren't going after your papi," he reiterated. "But his debt still stands. That's what matters. And that's where you come in, an able-bodied next of kin."

"Did he sign some sort of contract?"

"It was very much a contract. He worked his ass off to get your mom and little sister here. His bill is almost paid. Shouldn't be more than a few jobs."

Tony muttered to himself. Only the curse words were audible.

"If you don't respect our family, fine," Yadi said. "I get it. But for God's sake, respect your own. Honor your father. He wants a better life for all of you."

"Some of us didn't even have a father," Field cut in.

Yadi looked up at Field, impressed.

Tony looked down.

"So what you're saying is..." Yadi prompted Field.

Field took the cue.

"Be grateful, shut up, and get to work."

Yadi claimed those were words to live by.

Field only somewhat lived by them in the lucrative weeks that followed, fulfilling two-thirds of his own advice.

He was not grateful, but had already spent most of his life shutting up and working hard.

Aside from Tony, there were no independent accounts to oversee. He and Yadi still commuted together for the most part. But the pay was better. Field figured he must have been on some sort of provisional status during his previous time on the job, which sheltered him from the higher rewards until he had proven himself.

Maybe he was supposed to be grateful for their trust.

He did appreciate being able to give a lot of money to Lulu and her uncle. It was the most adult he had ever felt, based on the notion that adults work jobs they hate in order to take care of the most important people in their lives. Lulu's uncle was important for different reasons than Lulu, of course, reasons that prompted Field to refuse every invitation she offered to meet him. Field gave her his cell number with instructions to call him if she or her uncle ever needed anything, but every time he delivered some cash to their apartment building, she would invite him up to the second floor and he would decline.

One day she called to ask for a ride home from work.

She said the co-worker she was relying on had left early with a fever. Field was working with Yadi when he received the call, but agreed nonetheless, even though it meant driving back and forth between the two valleys after his shift was over.

"I'll be late," he apologized without telling her the logistics of why.

"It'll be worth the wait," she assured him.

"You're a good friend," Yadi told him as Field put the phone away.

"I'm all right," Field shrugged.

"She'd better be just as good a friend for you to give her that phone number," Yadi teased.

"She's the best."

Field was so sincere that Yadi dropped any further ribbing he may have been considering.

After a lap around some dismal households being held for ransom and a trip to the casino, Yadi suggested they give Lulu her ride home together before heading over the hills so Field wouldn't have to drive back.

"Thanks, Yadi, but I don't mind."

"That's a lot of driving."

"I want to keep my job away from her."

Yadi looked more hurt than Field could ever recall, which wasn't much, but more than he would ever expect.

"Sorry, Yadi."

"No. I get it."

They didn't exchange a word on the drive home, until Yadi dropped him off at the condo.

"Are you in love with this girl?" Yadi asked before Field could get out.

Field thought about it.

"I think it's a different kind of love than the one you're asking about," he said while looking through the windshield, trying to figure it out for himself as much as for Yadi. "I don't feel better about myself when I'm with her. I feel better about everyone else."

Yadi smiled.

"Then I guess you'd better go give her a ride home."

Field lifted his chin and stepped out of the truck.

He had never driven to Business Valley in the dark.

The abandoned station had no lights, so he couldn't see it.

But he could feel it. He always did. It was always there, somewhere in the darkness.

He wished someone would appear in his headlights and wave him down, having escaped from the station and fought their way to the roadside. That wasn't possible, though, because they hadn't delivered anyone there since the last time. He would know, since he was now fully invested in the company.

Lulu was waiting for him at the barbeque restaurant. The dinner crowd was sparse, not a crowd at all compared to the usual lunch rush. She leaned over the railing on the second floor and waved him up, where most of the tables were empty. There was a tired family of four in one corner, and a stoic older man in the other who was bundled up as though he had been in the fields.

Lulu gave Field a hug and guided him toward the table where the older man sat.

"I don't really need a ride," she confessed.

Field realized what was happening right before she introduced him.

"This is my uncle, Dante."

"Mucho gusto," Field said as he extended his hand.

Dante stood and shook it.

"The pleasure is mine," he replied in English with as much of an edge as an accent.

"I hope you're hungry," Lulu said to Field before her uncle could say anything else. "Tio is just starting to eat again, and get out of the house. I want to encourage both."

"This place is for tourists," Dante scoffed as they all sat down.

"Nobody visits here," Lulu reminded him.

"They are on their way to be tourists."

Field listened to Dante more than he could bear to look at him. His accent sounded heavier now that he had spoken more.

"Is chicken okay?" Lulu asked Field. "I ordered a platter."

"Fine. I really am hungry."

"Our treat," she offered.

Dante sounded like a tire that had sprung a leak.

"What?" she glared at him.

"It's his money," he gestured at Field.

"This is coming out of my check," she shot back.

"We can split it," Field suggested.

"No," Lulu insisted. "Besides, we have something to ask you."

"Another favor," Dante muttered.

"We're friends, sir," Field addressed him. "No such thing as a favor between us."

Dante looked at him and nodded before appearing to have problems of his own making eye contact.

Lulu smiled at Field.

"We have this project we're working on," she downshifted into a more serious tone. "A little memorial for Tia."

"I been working the fields forever," Dante wanted back in. "Seen so many people give their life to them. But no statues, no signs, nothing. You know, like at a school, or at a business or city hall, you know, how they have those things like that. This person, that person, they work here, now they're dead. Here they are, a statue of their head, a bench with their name on it. Like that."

Field studied him closely, then feared he may have been staring.

"We can't put up anything permanent," Lulu continued. "Pretty much all the farmland around here is privately owned, so we can't apply for any permits. Tio is a foreman and knows a lot of the owners. He was thinking of asking some for permission, but he's not comfortable asking just for Tia's sake, for one person."

"If we put up something like that," Dante said. "It should be for everyone. You know, like a war memorial, like those things on a battlefield that say there were soldiers here, and they died. Maybe we can do that someday, but right now I need a thing for my love. I need that first. And not like one of those crosses on the side of the road. Not like that. People will think there was a car accident or a tractor."

"So..." Lulu redirected the conversation. "What we were thinking is something solid and lasting, but underground. Like a time capsule, but not with a bunch of stuff. Just one thing. Show him, Tio."

Dante reached inside his jacket and produced a square, rusted piece of metal about the size of a paper napkin.

"Lulu she got this from her work," he said.

"I asked one of the sculptors, that woman from wine country, if she had any spare parts," Lulu explained.

"I try to write the name of my love on it," Dante held up the metal to reveal some words scratched on it.

Field tried to read the name.

"See?" Dante noticed. "Looks like shit. I try a nail, then a drill. But you can't read it."

"I can't read very well, anyway."

"Oh, Field," Lulu scolded him.

"I'm joking. Kind of."

"Sylvia," Dante said. "That was her name."

He looked at Field intently, or so Field thought. He wondered if Dante was toying with him. Maybe they both were.

"I've always liked that name," he told Dante, while telling himself that Dante would naturally look intense when talking about his wife who recently died.

Their number was announced. Lulu sprang up to fetch their order.

"Oh," she remembered. "What do you want to drink, Field?"

"I'll get it," he offered, eager to avoid sitting alone with Dante.

"Okay," she agreed. "But don't you dare pay for it."

Field didn't look back at him as they walked downstairs. He imagined Dante watching his every move, and hoped it was indeed his imagination.

"I haven't seen him this chatty since Tia disappeared," Lulu said as they reached the ground floor.

"Is that good?"

"It's great. He's getting back to being himself. Unless he was just tired of being around me all the time."

"He doesn't seem all that happy to be around me," Field unraveled his paranoia for inspection.

"Are you kidding?" she stopped before they reached the counter.

"I know he's talking, but he looks at me funny sometimes."

"He's uncomfortable about the money, like I told you he would be. But all this noise he's making, that's his way of thanking you."

"I hope so."

"It is. And he's going back to work after the ceremony, so he'll be a lot more relaxed around you once he's making his own money again."

She proceeded to the counter.

"Ceremony?" Field followed her.

She picked up the tray and ordered a drink for him. She waited until he received his cup to explain.

"For the name plate," she led him over to the drink station. "We're going to bury it in a field where she worked when she first got here."

"What's my role in this?"

He recognized the irony of his statement as he filled his cup with ice.

"We need an engraver."

Some ice cubes fell on the floor. Field kicked them under the machine.

"I don't know how to do that."

"I mean the tool," she smiled and clarified as the liquid gurgled into his cup. "We were hoping you could get us one from the store. Maybe even for a sweet deal, since you're a manager now."

She nudged him playfully.

"It would be my honor," he said as they headed back toward the stairs.

"Of course we want you to join us, too. Not just use you for the engraver."

"Join you for the ceremony?"

"Like I said, Tio is very grateful. Almost as grateful as I am."

She gave him a peck on the cheek before they started to climb back up.

As much as he dreaded going, the ceremony was beautiful.

They conducted it on a clear, cool day in a vacant field well off the nearest highway, a two-minute drive on a county road that stretched between a town of five thousand and a lettuce processing plant that was old enough and far enough away from where they stood to remind Field of the abandoned ranger station.

A small, deep hole had already been dug by the time he arrived. The hefty mound of black soil next to the narrow opening led him to deduce that someone had used an auger or a post digger to poke through the surface and dive deep enough to avoid the reach of the blades and discs that would mark the land and future.

Lulu's parents and siblings made up the majority of the small gathering. He hadn't seen them since graduation day. Each one of them gave him a hug. Her mother was last in the line, and she hugged him like she did when he was a child. He nearly confessed in her arms.

The inscription on the weathered metal square looked professional. Sylvia's name took up most of the space. Field assumed Lulu had been the one to handle the engraving. She confirmed it when he asked.

"You had another work of art in your after all," he told her.

She took his hand and squeezed it.

Most of the service was Uncle Dante speaking. All of it was in Spanish. He paused often to gather himself, determined not to break down. The last part of his speech overwhelmed him. He lost the fight. Field wondered if it was the words, or because he had reached the end and he couldn't fight anymore.

Lulu whispered in Field's ear.

"He wishes he could have been there with her during her last moments."

Field would have cried as well if he wasn't so scared that everyone knew: Lulu, Dante, their family, God.

His knees felt as though they were disappearing, leaving his legs to collapse. He barely managed to remain standing.

When Dante regained his composure, he knelt down to bury the metal plate. He filled the hole by hand. Field offered to help so that he had an excuse to lower himself to the ground. Dante waved him off, but Field fell to his knees anyway, trying to look useful, as though he was there in case.

He felt Lulu's hand rub his back as he watched the metal disappear into the earth. If the square had been clean and polished, it was the kind of piece he would be tempted to rub along his temple.

Dante rose and looked down at the freshly-disturbed patch. Field was about to stand, but Dante started to say a few more words in Spanish, so he remained on his knees. When Dante was done, he noticed Field still kneeling.

"This is not a lettuce field, or a pepper field," he translated. "It's a name field."

He returned to his first language. Field stood, keeping his eyes on the small grave. They joined hands in prayer. Field wouldn't have heard much even if he understood the words.

They had scheduled a barbeque in the small park that centered the nearby town, but Field said he had to be on his way. He made the announcement at a distance that kept him away from anymore hugs, except from Lulu. He waved his goodbyes instead. She escorted him to his car, and commented on what a lovely ceremony it was.

"Would you attend another ceremony with me?" he asked as they reached his car.

"That wrestling thing?"

"Yes."

"Of course."

"There's going to be some old classmates there," he warned her.

"They probably won't remember me."

He hugged her in gratitude and agreed to pick her up on the night in question.

The last home meet landed a couple of weeks before winter break, so none of their classmates who went away to college were in town yet. The crowd would be like most of the crowds at most of the meets, made up of those who never left, with a few more older locals than usual. Yadi decided it was best if he didn't attend. Field understood, and was all the more grateful to have Lulu to keep him company.

They didn't spend much time together in the gym. During the matches, there was a steady procession of people either shaking his hand, or leading him by it to another person or group waiting to pat him on the back or squeeze his shoulder. Lulu stayed on the bench in the bleachers next to the seat he vacated.

"Like high school all over again," she joked when he managed to make it back for what would probably not be for long.

"I'm sorry."

"I'm fine," she flapped a hand at him. "Soak it up. This is your night."

"Has anyone said 'hello' to you?"

"Your Mom."

Field appeared to lose feeling in his face.

"But I don't think she was sure who I was," she added.

"Is she with someone?" he asked.

"She wasn't when she passed by."

"Did you see where she went?" he looked intently at Lulu, afraid to look anywhere else.

"Not really. She never sat down."

"Of course not."

"She could be anywhere," Lulu acted like she was telling a ghost story.

Field smiled nearly to the point of laughter. He sat back to watch the match taking place. The two wrestlers were locked up to the point of being immobile. Field thought it would be easy to misunderstand their lack of movement if someone didn't understand the complexities involved. He was about to narrate what was happening between the two wrestlers for Lulu's sake.

"Field!"

His mother's voice made him quiver.

"Field," she called again over the crowd.

"Is she coming this way?" Field asked Lulu out the corner of his mouth.

"Yes."

He exhaled until she arrived.

"I thought that was you, Lulu!"

Lulu acknowledged her while Field stared at the match.

"You're so grown up," she kept talking to her, determined to draw Field's attention. "Your eyeballs look smaller."

"Shut up, Mom," he backed into her goal.

"Haven't seen you around, rock star," she replied as though he had simply said hello.

"I travel a lot for work," he kept his eyes on the match.

"Oh, really? Where to?"

"The valley."

"You earn mileage points for that?" she smirked.

"What are those?"

"You'd know if you ever flew on an airplane."

"I flew on an airplane to Colorado for the Olympic trials."

"I've been on a plane lots of times lately."

He finally looked at her.

"New boyfriend?"

"You should meet him."

"Is he here?"

"Out of town. Wished he could be."

"I'll bet."

"I know what you're gettin' at."

"Not tonight, Mom."

"He ain't fuckin' anyone else."

"Not tonight."

"Then when?"

"What?" Field started to raise his voice. "When can we fight?"

Lulu took his hand.

"Let's go visit the snack bar," she suggested.

But Field was now fixated on his mother.

"You miss this?" he controlled his volume but continued his interrogation. "This is how you think it's supposed to be?"

An aging fan wearing a high school letterman's jacket that he could no longer button thanks to his protruding belly approached Field.

"Congratulations, Field," the man reached out to shake his hand.

"Thank you, sir."

He stared at his mother while he removed his hand from Lulu's to accept the accolades.

His mother maintained her smirk.

"Can I get a picture?" the man asked.

"Of course," Field stood and looked away from his Mom long enough to lean in for a selfie with the fan.

"Thanks, Field. You were the best."

"You're welcome," he remained standing and resumed the staring contest with his mother as the man faded from view.

"You hear what he said?" she blinked.

"Yes."

"He said you *were* the best. Were."

"So?"

"You're not anymore."

Lulu stood and grabbed his hand more forcefully.

"Let's meet some more people who love you," she insisted.

Field settled down and silently agreed.

"Nice to see you again, Ms. Spahn," Lulu deadpanned as they left her behind.

They found further adoration within a few steps. Lulu let the crowd have him and found another seat. She spent the rest of the meet making sure his mother stayed away from him, which was easy, as she apparently left having felt she inflicted enough damage.

After the ritual of unveiling his name in the gym, there was a party thrown by a wealthy sponsor of the team who lived in a house that spread across a hill lined with vineyards that overlooked their hometown.

Field was the only member of his old team who was invited. The rest of the guests were business associates and local VIPs who started to compare success stories and complaints once the house was full of them, so Field and Lulu were able to escape out onto the deck without anyone noticing. They had the view to themselves, as the cold night air kept the proud alumni inside. The town was big enough to offer a show of lights, but small enough not to interfere with the display of stars in the sky. They spent some time figuring out which buildings were which now that they were seeing them from above for the first time, then looked up to see if they could remember the names of any constellations besides Orion.

"Was that weird?" Lulu asked him as they continued to star gaze. "Seeing your name up there, on the wall?"

"I don't think anything is weird anymore. Things just happen."

He looked at her.

"What about you?" he changed the subject. "Was that weird seeing all those people you didn't want to see anymore?"

"Not yet."

"Not yet?"

"They still look the same. It's only been a couple of years. It'll be more fun when they get old and fat."

The sliding glass doors opened behind them. They turned to see Gonzo enter from the snapshot of bodies framed in the background. Noise from their competing conversations were audible for a moment until he slid the door closed.

"Hope I'm not interrupting anything," he grinned.

"Just talking," Field assured him. "Looking at the view."

"We're not the only ones who live on this side of the hills and make our money on the other," Gonzo joined them at the railing. "This guy is big in the cotton industry. He makes wine from these vines on his property just for fun."

"Gonzo," he didn't want to talk business. "Have you ever met Lulu?"

"I don't believe I have."

"I thought so," Field said as he stepped back so the two of them could greet each other. "We were best friends in elementary school, then, well, I got into wrestling."

"I'm sorry," Gonzo chuckled as he extended a hand to Lulu. "Pleasure to meet you, dear."

"Likewise," Lulu shook it. "He never mentioned me?"

"He was very focused."

"I was full of myself," Field pled guilty.

"You had every reason to be proud of yourself," Gonzo lent him an excuse.

Field glanced self-consciously at Lulu, whose coy look verged on reassuring.

"If you two were so close in elementary school," Gonzo continued. "Does that mean you were Special Ed buddies?"

"That's one way to put it," Lulu granted.

"Well, then," Gonzo was delighted. "You both have a lot to be proud of. You're an inspiration to kids going through the same things you did."

"I guess," Field was genuinely unsure.

"Absolutely," Gonzo patted him on the back. "Hey, did I see your mother there tonight?"

"You did."

"Almost didn't recognize her. How is she?"

"Her voice is the same."

Lulu contributed a rueful snort.

Gonzo hummed in understanding before laying the groundwork for his exit.

"It's an honor, Lulu. Thanks for taking such good care of him until we got our hands on him."

"I didn't have much choice," she said. "None of our other classmates could speak."

Gonzo erupted in laughter.

"Razor sharp," he said to Field while nodding in Lulu's direction. "You'd never know."

Field and Lulu glared at one another. Gonzo was oblivious.

"I'll leave you two alone," he excused himself. "I just needed to get some cool air. Nothing but the hot stuff in there. Don't leave without saying goodbye."

"Will do," Field waved as Gonzo headed back in. They watched him slide the door open and shut, turning the noise on and off with it.

"You'd never know?" Lulu rehashed Gonzo's line.

"Well..." Field paused. "You wouldn't."

"Do I have to explain why that was offensive?"

"No. I get it. But still..."

"Don't make me hit you. For real."

"Be proud," he held up his hands. "He's right about that. You are an inspiration."

"And you're not?"

"Yeah, right. Hey kids, your disabilities won't hold you back, as long as you're good at a sport."

"Or if you're not good at a sport," she piggybacked on his message. "You can be like me. Work hard, get mainstreamed, and someday you can drop out of college."

"You have those credits, or units. Whatever they're called. You can probably do something with those. Be a tutor, like the people who used to work with us in the small group sessions."

Lulu appeared to mull the possibility as she took in the view once again, unobstructed by Gonzo's presence.

"He seemed to think there was something between us," she said.

"There is."

He joined her in looking back at where they grew up.

"Did you ever think about kissing me?"

Field reeled a bit, as though the view of their town was spinning.

"I'm not suggesting anything," she assured him. "I'm just curious."

"I wondered what it was like to kiss just about every girl in school."

"*Just about* every girl?"

"I was a boy."

"That's not what I meant."

"Oh..." he elongated the word in recognition. "*Just about* included you."

"Thanks."

"You're welcome."

He looked at her longer than she expected.

"No," she said.

"What?"

"I said I didn't mean anything by asking."

"I'm not..."

"I'm kidding," she slugged him.

They settled once more into the silence of the sights above and below.

"But you did look at me a long time just then."

Field exhaled a groan while Lulu laughed.

"Everyone compliments us for having some sort of unique story," she said once their noises subsided. "But now that we've overcome our situations, our whatevers, we're pretty normal when it comes to what people aren't looking for in love."

"I'm not sure what you mean, and I'm not sure I want you to explain."

"We're stereotypes of what disappoints people. I'm a woman without enough looks, and you're a man who has too much of them."

"And not enough smarts."

"I was thinking career prospects," she defended herself. "I was going to say money, but that's not necessarily true."

Field nodded dolefully.

"I'm sorry," Lulu said. "That didn't come out the way I wanted it to."

"That's okay," he kept nodding.

She turned her gaze forward but fidgeted, thinking of some way to change the subject or apologize further without actually apologizing again.

"It was embarrassing," he broke the silence before she could.

"I said I was sorry."

"No," he continued to look out over the valley with their town at the bottom of it. "Not that. The Ring of Honor."

She was relieved he wasn't referring to what she said, but still needed to comfort him.

"You made people happy."

"People who rooted for me. I made other people sad."

"It's just wrestling, Field. It's a sport."

He looked above the lights of their town to the darkness beyond that hovered above the valley where he made money, where he made people unhappy. His eyes adjusted to the night sky and he started to make out the ridgeline of the hills that separated one valley from the other. He imagined they were above and below each other, rather than side by side, and that he was looking down at it rather than across.

He was due in the valley below in two days, scheduled to pay Tony a visit after a day off following the Ring of Honor festivities.

Tony was staying out of the crack houses by working in the fields. Yadi had a lead on which crew Tony was working with, so they went out as a team in spite of the initial plan for Field to handle his account individually. They had the number of a bus and a general location of the field Tony's crew was scheduled to service.

As they commuted back to business in Yadi's truck, he asked Field how the ceremony went, and the party afterwards.

Field kept replying "Fine," like a child whose parent was asking him about his day at school.

"I couldn't risk running into any clients or former clients," Yadi explained again.

"It's not that."

"It was a small chance," Yadi pursued his defense. "Not much crossover between the valleys, but it was a chance we couldn't take."

"I get it."

"*We*," he disabled the word. "Gonzo's been behind the scenes so long, he can get away with working a room. The business was small-time back when he was out in front."

"Are you not listening to me?"

"I am. I just need to hear my excuses out loud. Make sure they sound good. I was bummed, man. I really wanted to be there."

"Thanks, Yadi. But really, I didn't want to be there. That's why I'm not saying much."

"Compartmentalize," he reached over and massaged Field's shoulder for a second.

"I don't think that word means anything."

"It means putting some stuff over here, and other stuff over there. Usually business stuff and personal stuff."

"I mean nobody can really do it. They only think they can."

"I don't know about that."

"I had a long talk with Lulu," Field stiff-armed the conversation. "I don't need to dump anymore on anyone else. It was a nice ceremony. They did a good job. Too bad it was for me."

Some old school buses painted white that towed trailers topped with porta-potties were parked alongside a vineyard as wide and flat as a lake. The field was devoted to table grapes rather than wine grapes, so the plants had longer, leafier vines that looked like waves as they bobbed in the breeze.

"I think this might be us," Yadi announced as they slowed down by the vineyard's edge and parked in back of the buses.

Few of the workers were visible, scattered inside the jungle of grape leaves. Yadi and Field approached one of the foremen who had set up shop at a folding table weighted down by a Gatorade dispenser with "Agua" handwritten across it in black ink.

The foreman spoke English, and waved them in the direction where he thought there may be a young man fitting Tony's description.

"Oh well," Yadi said to Field as they headed for the likely rows. "I guess you didn't need me here after all."

"At least we can cover more ground."

"I'll take the far ones. You can take the ones closer to the bus."

They split up.

Most of the workers looked older. Field wasn't sure if they really were, or if they were weather-beaten. He acknowledged those who glanced his way as he crept down each aisle, sweeping aside vines with his forearm. He felt as though he should have been wielding a machete to clear his path, and that a towering stone temple would eventually reveal itself beyond the foliage, rising above the forest.

"Field!" Yadi's voice put him back in the present. "I got him!"

He turned and swam back through the flora. The workers wore more concerned expressions on his return trip.

By the time he emerged into the open, many of them had also decided to follow Yadi's call to see what was happening.

Tony stood placidly by Yadi.

"Save me, G.G.," Tony huffed. "I don't care what the job is, I'd rather be arrested than spend another minute out here."

"I wish it was always this easy," Yadi chuckled.

"You're welcome," Tony said.

He walked over to the foreman's table and raised his pruning shears to eye level before dropping them onto the table top.

"You wanna tell him about his assignment?" Yadi asked Field.

"Sure," Field turned and prepared to greet Tony on his return from the table show.

Before Tony reached conversation distance, Field noticed one of the workers in the background standing with his arms crossed rather than by his side like the others.

Then he noticed it was Lulu's uncle.

"So what's the gig?" Tony asked.

Field was too distracted by Dante's stare.

"G.G.?" Tony tried to get his attention.

Field shed his focus from Dante and shot it at Tony.

"Don't call me that," he growled.

"Sorry," Tony reared back.

"You think it's funny?" Field kept after him, reaching an intensity almost as ferocious as the one emanating from Dante.

"Whoa, Field," Yadi stepped up beside him.

"You're a fucking junkie," Field wasn't done. "You don't have the right to laugh at anyone."

"Why don't I tell him about the job," Yadi guided him away from Tony. "And you chill out."

Field followed orders, but was breathing heavily as he took his place to the side. He avoided looking at Dante, but could see him approaching while Yadi spoke with Tony.

When Dante reached him, Field still couldn't manage to make eye contact. Dante simply stood and dared him to look or speak.

"I thought you were a foreman," Field tried to keep the conversation small.

"I need to work a little bit first," he indulged Field's attempt. "It takes time to get back to normal when you have something so terrible happen."

Field saw no point in further pretense.

"I knew it," Dante accepted Field's surrender. "I knew it was you they talk about. But I like the money too much, so I look away."

Field thought about how he could relate to that condition, and would have said so, but didn't feel as though he had the right to compare himself to Dante, no more right than Tony had to laugh at anyone.

"You want to hit me?" he asked instead.

Dante looked confused.

"Hit me," Field implored. "Free shot, right here in front of everyone."

Dante appeared to consider it, but held back.

"No," he decided.

"Why not?"

"Because you want me to."

They stared at each other while some of the workers started to gather around them.

Dante snapped the silence.

"You can never see my niece again."

Field was afraid he might cry in front of everyone.

"You don't want me to do that?" Dante taunted him.

Some tears mounted along his lids and before they could fall, Field camouflaged them by taking Dante down and pinning his face to the ground.

"I will do," he hissed in Dante's ear, "whatever the fuck I want to do."

Yadi slid his hands under Field's arms, pressed the back of his head, and rolled him off of Dante. Field was stuck flailing like a turtle teetering upside down on its shell as Yadi held him from behind.

"We have no more business with this man," Yadi grunted into Field's ear. "His debt is paid."

Field cursed and brayed at Yadi, searching for a way to get out of the hold and return some punishment.

"This is your fault!" Field started to wear down. "You did this to me!"

"I'm sorry," Yadi did his best to sound consoling. "We need to go now."

"I'm not going anywhere with you. I'm done."

"I understand. We can talk."

"No!" Field found another burst of energy. "I always lose when I talk!"

"Don't make me choke you out."

Field knew Yadi had the leverage, and could feel him start to use it. He went slack and tapped Yadi on the arm.

"No tricks?" Yadi asked.

Field murmured a resignation.

Yadi released him.

They sat covered in dirt, catching their breath. Field stared at the dust clouds dissipating between them rather than risk seeing how large the crowd had become. He saw Yadi rise to his feet, but didn't follow him.

"I'll be back, Tony," he heard him say.

"You're gonna leave me here?" Tony whined.

"Just for a while."

Tony groaned.

"Field?" Yadi asked, as though trying to wake him up.

"Field?" he repeated. "Come on. I'll take you home."

Field slowly made his way onto two feet. He focused on Yadi's truck, and nothing else, as he walked toward it.

When they drove away, he caught a glimpse of Lulu's uncle through the window.

In his eyes Field saw the rusted metal tower, and his wife inside of it. He saw her eyes. They were pleading, like they always did. Now there were two pairs of eyes, like there always would be.

"What was that about a niece?" Yadi asked after they had been on the road a while.

"Nothing. He's a crazy old man."

"He's a lot of things, but he's not crazy. What's your connection?"

"I gave his wife a ride one day," Field said with uncharacteristic detachment.

"We shifted our efforts to his wife after you started working for us."

"Shifted our efforts..."

"You were never with me when I visited him," Yadi clarified.

Field wished he could come up with a story, but had neither the drive nor the talent.

"He's Lulu's uncle."

"Lulu, that girl friend of yours?" Yadi confirmed. "That girl who's a friend?"

"The best friend."

He heard himself describe their relationship and it sounded like a memory.

He saw the concern on Yadi's face as he looked ahead at what was coming.

They were the two people closest to him that he wanted to keep close, and he may have lost them both on the same trip.

Maybe he felt I was the only one left with any sort of bond to the person he hoped he still was. Then again, I was the only person he knew whose job it was to deal with problems in life. A child's life, but those problems still tended to involve adults.

Whatever the reason, he came to my office soon after Yadi dropped him off, and he told me everything. We met once or twice a day for a week. I listened, comforted him, and when he was finished, encouraged him to alert the authorities.

"I told you about where I got my car," he reminded me. "Some of the police are in on it. I don't know which ones, or if they're sheriff's department or local police in any of the towns. I don't know who to trust."

"There are other agencies you can contact."

He didn't ask what they were. He didn't say anything for a while.

"I'm part of it," he said at last. "I'd be turning myself in."

"They would probably strike a deal with you."

"It wouldn't even get that far. Someone would kill me first."

It was my turn to fall silent.

"I just wanted to talk," he said. "Please don't say anything to anyone."

"It's not my decision, Field. It's up to you."

He paused again before thanking me for listening.

He accused me of doing more than that when a federal investigator approached him days later with questions he refused to answer.

I assured him I didn't call anyone.

He wondered aloud who did.

I asked him if that's what really mattered.

He refused to answer my question as well.

# CHAPTER EIGHT: RECKONING

Lulu threatened to scream when he visited her at the shop.

"Not another step," she warned him.

They stood in an aisle filled with souvenirs that had no specific references to the valley in which they were sold. The closest any came had "California" on them, while the rest offered inspirational quotes, or jokes about getting old.

"I might scream anyway," she followed up.

"I'm sorry," he begged. "A million times, I'm sorry. I'll even say it a million times, actually say it, if you want me to."

"I want you to leave. My uncle said he forbid you from seeing me. I told him that wasn't necessary. I could make that decision on my own."

"Did you call the feds?

"The feds? That doesn't sound very gangster."

"Well, did you?"

"Did you kill my aunt?"

"No."

"Did you have anything to do with her disappearance?"

Field wasn't sure how to answer.

"I'll take that as a 'yes,'" she said.

"It's not that simple, Lulu."

"You either had something to do with it, or you didn't."

"There's layers," he worked on an answer out loud. "All these steps, so everyone can say they didn't do it, whatever the big thing is."

Lulu was surprised to hear him acknowledge that much. She froze in between her anger and sadness.

"What was your step?" she asked.

Field hesitated long enough to give her the impression he might provide an answer.

"I can't answer that," he let her down.

"Yes, you can."

"I don't want to."

She sized him up.

"So that's it?"

He nodded.

"Then like I said before, we're done."

She turned and walked away.

"You weren't even that close to her," he stopped her within two steps.

She pivoted and glared at him.

"You said so," he reminded her. "You barely knew her."

"What difference does that make?"

"You know me way better than you knew her."

"You're such an idiot."

"Don't call me that."

"Idiot!" she yelled. "Dummy! Moron!"

"Stop it!" he yelled back.

"Or what?" she matched him. "What are you gonna do? Take some steps? But that's not your decision, is it? You just follow orders."

The store manager surfaced at the head of aisle.

"Seriously?" she berated them. "You're lucky nobody else is in here."

She shook her head and expelled some air before submerging back to the counter.

Lulu and Field looked anywhere but at each other.

"Did you call the authorities?" he tried one last time.

She busied herself with some mugs on a nearby shelf, lining them up so the handles all faced the same direction. He waited to see how long she could keep pretending he wasn't there. When she moved on to a rack of sweatshirts to make sure each size was grouped together in the same category, he asked again.

She answered without looking away from her self-imposed task.

"We both have a secret now," she said.

Neither was much of a secret, Field gathered.

Gonzo and Yadi also assumed she had spurred the investigation rather than her uncle, who would have done so much earlier, but never did because he knew firsthand how their business was conducted. Field clenched when they shared their mutual suspicions during a meeting in Gonzo's office while business operations were in limbo, suspended indefinitely by order of the family executives. He had visions of being asked to deliver Lulu and her uncle to the station, or even eliminating a step by taking care of the situation himself as a test of loyalty.

But neither Gonzo nor Yadi seemed concerned.

"It'll blow over," Gonzo said from behind his desk.

"It always does," added Yadi as he leaned in the corner closest to the window that overlooked the home store floor.

Their nonchalance helped Field relax.

"When you merge with the kind of business we did a few years back, it comes with the territory," Gonzo explained.

"Like the occasional arrest," Yadi offered another recent example.

"It never gets very far," Gonzo said. "They'll deport some people. Some of them customers, so we'll lose that money, but they don't bother with anything beyond immigration. Too complicated. That's another advantage of the merger. The family's network is so complex that it's hard to build a case against it. And it mostly affects illegals, so nobody cares."

"I know it's rocked your world," Yadi acknowledged Field's dismay. "But look around. You won't find any stories about Lulu's aunt in the local news, no fliers posted in store windows or on fence posts."

"Not a whole lot of pressure on anyone to solve this case," Gonzo said.

"They only sent one guy this time," Yadi noted. "At least I think it's only one. Who talked to you, Field? Was it Agent...uh, what's his name?"

"Barajas?"

"That's it," Yadi snapped. "Agent Barajas talk to you yet, Gonzo?"

"Nope. Thanks to you two."

"Agent Barajas isn't very persuasive," Yadi brushed off the compliment. "Is he, Field?"

"I guess not," he shrugged.

"Speak for yourself, Yadi," Gonzo said. "He doesn't have anyone to compare him to. All the more reason to be impressed with the teamwork. As far as Field is concerned, he's the most intimidating agent he's ever ever met."

He started to laugh, followed by Yadi, then Field, in successive order of glee.

"Plus you have that personal connection to the victim," Gonzo said as the laughter died.

Field stopped before Yadi.

"It's a compliment," Gonzo assured him. "Not a threat. You held him off in spite of all these factors working against you."

"And it is a strong connection," Yadi jumped back in.

"Have you met Lulu?" Gonzo asked him.

"Actually, I haven't. I just pulled Field off her uncle."

They started laughing again, but Field didn't succeed in joining them this time.

"Wonderful girl," Gonzo said. "I definitely understand the appeal."

"I didn't say anything," Field was compelled to remind them.

"Did Agent Balboa, or Borges, whatever, did he try to use your feelings for Lulu against you?" Gonzo asked.

"No."

"He will," Gonzo leaned forward. "Even if he's the worst agent in the field, he's been given a gift. There's never been a bridge between our side and the customers' side. They might actually care about a case out here if they think they can solve it."

"It won't matter," Field felt his voice tremble.

Gonzo stared at him for a while before speaking again.

"You've also been given a gift," he said. "You're able to see how the world works. Everyone knows that someone down the line is paying a price for our happiness. The all-you-can-eat buffet, the bargain rack. On the other end of that production is someone who's very unhappy. You not only know that, you get it. You know who those people are. You work with them. And that makes you better than the average person, Field. Your awareness puts you above the rest. You can truly appreciate what you have. Don't throw that away. What do we owe a childhood friend? Everyone gets so poetic when it comes to that time of life, but there's a reason we grow apart. We don't know who we are when we're kids. How well can we know someone else when we don't know ourselves?"

Field wasn't sure he agreed with Gonzo, but he was able to follow his point, which always felt good in a lifetime of usually feeling lost.

"We're going to keep things quiet for a while longer," Gonzo said after another pause long enough to make Field think he was referring to his speech pattern. "We'll wait until Agent B's boss decides to make a show of deporting a few poor souls, or just calls him off. And when we're back in business, you're welcome back out in the field, or if you prefer, you can stay on in more of a white collar position."

"Without even having to wear a tie," Yadi quipped.

"Oh, so that's what white collar means," Field realized.

Gonzo and Yadi enjoyed Field's insight before Gonzo introduced the offer.

"How would you like to get into real estate?"

"Like Yadi?"

"Even more than me," Yadi said. "Better."

"We've got our eye on three different buildings," Gonzo explained. "Each in a different town, including some commercial space next to The Crossroads Center. Maybe give them a run for their money if we attract the right clients."

"You need my name."

"We need you," Gonzo was quick to counter.

"There's a new real estate agent in the area who's a fan of yours," Yadi said. "He wrestled at Fresno State and thinks it's a shame you never got the same chance. He'd probably be willing to talk the sellers down to half their asking price if you asked him to."

"Yadi's only half-exaggerating. And whatever percentage below the list price you can get us on each building, you take home that percentage of the rent we collect every month."

Field struggled to sort out the deal.

"Shall we do some math?" Gonzo asked. "Show you what that might look like?"

"I'm not sure I want to know," Field hedged.

"It's overwhelming," Gonzo commiserated.

"I also had some ideas of my own on what I might do."

"Really?"

"Yes."

Gonzo and Yadi waited for an answer that Field wasn't giving them. They looked at each other and decided Yadi should ask.

"Well," he said. "What's on your mind, Field?"

"I was thinking maybe I'd move."

"Out of the condo?" Gonzo wanted to know.

"Out of town."

Gonzo and Yadi exchanged glances again.

"To where?" Yadi asked.

"A big city with lots of people and jobs. San Francisco or Los Angeles, maybe even farther. Some place where I can disappear and start over."

"With what skills?" Gonzo pressed him.

Yadi appeared more sympathetic and briefly scowled at Gonzo behind his back.

"I haven't thought that much about it," Field admitted.

"Clearly," Gonzo snorted.

"Big cities are expensive," Yadi added out of concern.

"A job as a bouncer ain't gonna cut it," Gonzo stuck with scorn. "You'll make a great homeless person, though. You can scare people into giving you money."

Field failed to hide his embarrassment.

"It's just a thought," he virtually whispered.

"Well think more about what we offered. It's a once in a lifetime opportunity. No bullshit. That's the truth."

"I know," Field bowed his head. "Thank you."

"Take some time over the holidays to look into the future. Think of the new year as more than just a new year."

"I will."

"It's a new life. Or at least, it can be."

Field stopped responding.

"Say the word," Gonzo kept punching, "and I'll set up an appointment with that agent."

"The real estate agent," Yadi tried to ease the tension. "Not the federal agent."

Field pushed a smile through his daze.

He tried again when the federal agent intercepted him outside the condo.

Agent Barajas had followed him home.

Field noticed him in the rearview mirror about a mile before they reached the parking spaces, so he was able to rehearse a calm demeanor, which he knew would be hard to maintain once he stepped outside.

"I told you everything I know," he didn't even try.

"Which was exactly nothing," Barajas said, shutting his car door for emphasis. He looked like he was there to secure the area for a visit from the president.

"I'm not a very important part of whatever you think is going on," Field stayed by his car.

"I could get the courts involved," Barajas came around and stood where Field would have to pass through to reach his front door. "Force you to talk."

"That would be a waste of time."

"Or we could just talk about Lulu."

Field expected Barajas to revel in his leverage somehow, with a smile or crossed arms, but he remained stoic.

"What about her?" Field asked.

"Let's take a walk," he suggested. "Condos share walls."

He stepped aside, and Field led him down a path between the units to the greenbelt that stretched behind the complex, where a paved trail lined with occasional barbeque areas and playgrounds ambled along the banks of a dry creek shrouded in cottonwood and sycamore trees. Roughly a third of their leaves still clung to their branches, while the others had fallen to form a yellow, brown, and red carpet that changed its pattern with each ripple in the current of the airstream.

"Nice," Barajas nodded at the surroundings as they walked through them. "Anyone use the barbeques or playgrounds?"

Field shook his head.

"Mostly old people walking their dogs," he said.

"That's pretty much the whole town, as far as I can tell."

"Yeah," Field couldn't help but chuckle.

"It's expensive to live here."

Field's cheer gave way to a sigh.

"Maybe they'll buy you a dog next," Barajas continued.

They kept walking.

"Isn't that what they do?" he pressed. "Buy you things?"

Field wasn't sure whether to walk faster or slower. Barajas settled the conundrum by stopping.

"What can your old friend possibly offer?" he asked.

He took in the trees and a deep breath, as though Field wasn't there and he was talking to himself.

"What can she give you that you don't already have? Morals? Value? Purpose?"

He looked at Field.

"You already have those, don't you?"

Field didn't look at him.

"Don't you?" he asked again.

Field started walking back to the complex.

Barajas didn't follow.

"You have my card," he called after him.

Field raised his arm in acknowledgement without turning or breaking stride.

"Merry Christmas, Field."

He stayed in the condominium straight through the holidays, ordering one meal a day and staring out the windows. Sometimes he would realize he had been staring at a wall, or the ceiling. He had never spent so much time inside of it. He watched videos on his phone that had nothing to do with Christmas, so he would merely feel alone, rather than alone for the holidays. His favorite were animal rescues.

Some he watched repeatedly, like the one of a whale being untangled from a fishing net by divers and people navigating inflatable boats. He thought he recognized the background music from his old *Symphony of the Ocean* CD he had won for answering a question correctly on their field trip to the aquarium. Years had passed since he was able to listen it, so he wasn't certain. He was surprised he couldn't remember the melody better, given how often he played it, and thought perhaps the whale sounds from the CD were crafting a false memory of the music thanks to the sight of the whale on the video.

He also liked the orphaned lioness cub who was found and raised by a ranger on a game reserve, who ran up to hug the ranger every time she saw him out in the wild after she was grown up and released. Field wondered if the ranger ever got nervous as she charged him, thinking maybe it was some other lioness, but apparently he could always tell it was her.

A call on his cell woke him.

He wasn't sure if he was being stirred from a nap or a night's sleep, and the gray light coming through the windows from the winter cloud cover offered no clues. It was only when he saw the time on his screen that was able to conclude it was morning.

Yadi's voice greeted him when he answered.

"Happy New Year, Champ."

"Happy New Year."

"Look, I know it's a nice condo, but you might get sick of it if you don't get out once in a while."

"Have you been tracking me?"

"You haven't been at the store, you haven't been in the field, and hanging out with Lulu's family is about as much of an option now as hanging out with your own family."

"True."

"Plus you earned a bunch of pizza points that keep coming up on my phone. Same network, remember?"

"Oh. Sorry."

"So let's get out. I've got an appointment with our new realtor, Nate. He wants to give us a tour of the buildings. Mostly I think he wants to meet you."

"I don't know."

Yadi sighed, then emerged from it irritated.

"You're not still thinking of leaving town, are you?"

"Maybe."

"Come on, Field. You've got a chance to be the most successful person in your high school class before the rest of them even finish college. Who could have seen that coming? Even if you kept wrestling, news flash, there's not much money in real wrestling."

"Okay," Field felt uncomfortable hearing him beg. "Fine."

"Yes!" Yadi let out a verbal fist pump. "I'll come pick you up in an hour. Nate's treating us to lunch. Wear your high school wrestling hoodie, and when he asks to take a selfie with you, just go with it."

Nate was dressed and groomed like a World Cup soccer player holding a press conference, though his blazer looked too small rather than tailored. He asked for that selfie before they went inside a franchise bar and grill he had suggested, which was in one of the larger cities in the valley, dozens of miles from the territories Field and Yadi usually covered.

The first property they visited after lunch was within the same sprawling city limits. It was in as much need of repair as the ones Gonzo owned in the rural areas. The dust and grit that clung to the walls in the city was darker in color than its country counterpart, and Field couldn't decide if being surrounded by sprawl rather than absence made the structure more depressing or less.

"Do any farmworkers live here?" Field asked.

Yadi answered before Nate.

"We're considering expanding into other industries. The urban labor market is something we can't afford to ignore much longer."

The other properties were on ground that was more familiar.

Field had never noticed the commercial spread near The Crossroads. It was a small strip mall half-inhabited by a check-cashing service and a donut shop.

"At the very least we'll be able to shut down the check-cashing business," Yadi winked at Field.

Meanwhile, Nate talked more about wrestling than real estate in proportion to the condition of each site they toured. The more dilapidated the building, the more he reminisced about his matches or Field's, several of which he had caught when Field's high school team traveled inland.

As they stood outside their final stop, which looked like no one was living in it if not for the occasional face peering out from behind the bath towels and bed sheets that served as curtains, Nate claimed he had wanted to personally recruit Field to his alma mater, but their athletic director didn't approve the visit.

"Grades aren't everything," he said. "I tried to tell him college would have a lot more resources to help someone like you."

"It didn't do my best friend much good," Field thought of Lulu.

"Yet here we are," Yadi cut in. "Building an empire."

Nate and Yadi exchanged an aggressive handshake and hug.

"We'll be in touch," Yadi told him.

"Definitely," Nate said, then turned to Field.

"An absolute pleasure," he extended his hand. "I may not have gotten the chance to wrestle with you, but look forward to doing business with you."

Field shook his hand and made the most conciliatory noise he could muster.

On their way back west, Yadi seemed to want to berate Field, but tried his best to maintain a soft touch.

"We're thinking of turning the commercial spot into a hotel," he pitched. "So the initial returns wouldn't be great, but long term, it'll be a gold mine. We'd be the only hotel there."

Field watched the countryside roll toward the hills looming ahead.

"I didn't want to say too much in front of Nate," Yadi continued. "He's eager, but he needs to earn our trust a little more."

Field stopped even his barely perceptible responses. He thought of the faces in the windows of the last building they had circled.

"Meanwhile, the residential units will provide plenty of cash flow."

"I'm sorry," Field snapped out of his trance. "I can't."

Yadi took a deep breath, appearing to calm himself down rather than register disappointment.

"Please think more carefully about this."

"What do you think I've been doing the past couple weeks?"

"Making the wrong decision," Yadi raised his voice.

Field glared at him.

"I mean," Yadi backtracked. "Did you even give it a chance? Did you consider any of the good things? Or just think about the bad parts over and over again?"

"I have a hard time getting past the bad parts," Field admitted.

"Then try harder," Yadi pleaded.

"What's the big deal?" Field asked. "I'm leaving town. I won't cause any problems."

Yadi laughed the kind of laugh that comes when all other forms of emotion have been exhausted.

"You should see the guy I have to work with if you leave."

"Then come with me," Field seized a chance. "Remember when you told me about Disneyland and places like that? How the people in costume work in pairs?"

"Oh, God. You're kidding."

"Let's do it!" Field was excited. "Let's get jobs at Disneyland. We can get paid to wear disguises."

Yadi laughed for real, but not for long.

Field didn't want to let the moment go.

"I'm serious."

"So am I," Yadi replied.

Field looked back out the window and saw his disappointment reflected in the winter sparseness.

"We have to make one last stop," Yadi announced.

Field didn't respond.

Yadi took out his phone and tapped a quick message.

They took the last exit before the climb into the hills, the same one they took when they bought Field's car. As they turned in the direction of the police impound lot, Field thought maybe they were going to make arrangements to take the car back.

"You get to meet your replacement," Yadi explained as they sped through the remoteness that buffered the approaching fences. "Think you can stick around long enough to help me train him?"

"Sure," Field shrugged.

"Gonzo wants me to show him the abandoned station first. Start with the worst-case scenario so everything else seems easy."

"If you had done that with me, I never would have joined."

"If you didn't know that woman's family, it wouldn't have mattered."

Yadi took his turn as the unresponsive one. He kept his eyes on the chain link fence as it filed past, in anticipation of the gate.

Field's first instinct of being offended by Yadi's claim started to fade as he considered whether he really would have been able to move on from that delivery without someone close to him being affected. By the time they reached the entrance, he had progressed from protest to contemplation.

The gate was open this time. Yadi turned into the lot and the same testy mechanic who had served them was standing near the first row of vehicles. He was talking to someone who had his back to them.

When he turned around, Yadi told Field that was his replacement.

If the idea was to hire someone who could handle worse-case scenarios, his replacement appeared to be ideal. He looked worse than mean. He looked like he didn't care, with a slightly-open mouth and expressionless eyes that would likely be unmoved by the great violence he was clearly capable of.

"I'll get in the back seat," Field climbed between the front seats. He didn't want the man with the shark eyes behind him.

Yadi said nothing of it. He pulled up to the mechanic and the replacement and lifted his fingers off the steering wheel in a wave while maintaining his grip. The replacement let himself in the passenger side.

"This is Enrique," Yadi introduced him.

Field replied with a low "what's up".

Enrique glanced over his shoulder and either nodded at Field or looked him over.

They drove in silence for the most part. The rare speaking parts were in Spanish. Their longest exchange occurred when they made the turn onto the carved road that led up to the station. Field thought they sounded like a couple arguing over directions, which nearly made him giggle at how unlikely that was, given their machismo and there being only one route to their destination.

He was surprised that the slow ride through the gullies and tiers didn't elicit more haunting flashbacks to the last time they ambled along the crackling surface. Maybe he was cut out for this business after all, but he didn't want to be.

After they parked and walked toward the tower, Field expected the dialogue to pick up, as Yadi explained to Enrique the history and purpose of the site. But they remained quiet, the crunching of their footsteps the sole sound.

When they entered the building, Yadi and Enrique looked around, but separately. A light breeze passed through the cracks in the walls on one side and out the cracks in the other.

"Yadi?" Field wanted to offer to conduct the tour if the tension between the two of them was in the way. "Does Enrique speak some English?"

Yadi turned to face him and appeared to be in tears.

Field didn't want Yadi to look weak in front of Enrique, so he tried to cover for him by following through on his offer.

"I'll show him around."

Yadi looked in Enrique's direction.

Field did the same.

Enrique was pointing a gun at Field.

Field looked back at Yadi, whose breathing was labored from holding back his tears.

"Last chance," he managed to say. "Take the deal, Field. For the love of God, take the deal."

Enrique started walking toward Field to make his job easier.

Field backpedaled away from him at the same pace.

"Yadi?" he didn't know what else to say. "Yadi?"

His back was almost to the door when Enrique started to close the gap between them and put Yadi behind him.

"Take it!" Yadi yelled from several paces in the background.

"Yadi…"

"Take it!"

Enrique raised his pistol.

Yadi yelled one more time, but rushed Enrique as he did.

He tackled him in a bear hug, clamping down on his arms at the moment of impact, forcing him to fumble the gun, then rolled him over and pinned him while the pistol spun near the struggle.

"Run!" Yadi screamed.

Field hesitated, looking for a way to help Yadi.

"Run!" Yadi repeated.

Field lunged toward them.

"No!" Yadi ordered.

Field grabbed the gun off the floor and ran out the door.

He ran around to the side of the tower that faced west, toward home, and treaded down the hill as fast as he could without tumbling. The highway was far enough to the side that the vehicles looked like toys on a track, but he wanted to be nowhere near a road, so he veered diagonally down the grade away from civilization, waving the gun as he flapped his arms to keep his balance.

His knees burned with resistance by the time he reached flat ground. He looked behind him up the hill and could see the top of the tower, so he ran in spite of his exhaustion. He ran without having to brace himself against a fall, ran unfettered so fast that his knees loosened up. The world was nothing but his limbs, lungs, and heart pumping, heavy gulps of cold air fueling the motion and keeping time, as though he was in training to wrestle once again.

He came upon a vineyard that had been cleared. Piles of vines ripped from the ground were stacked several feet high in random spots for hundreds of acres, some of them on fire. The twisted roots that had been upended were wet, so they produced more smoke than flame. What flares did rise stood out dramatically against the grayscale background projected by a thick January sky. A controlled burn meant there would be workers to monitor it, so Field slowed down and buried the gun in the pocket of his wrestling hoodie. His breathing had normalized by the time he passed by a couple of men who inspected one of the hissing masses. They glanced his way and he waved at them. They waved back and returned to their work, entranced by one of their enormous campfires.

When he had passed through the burn piles, Field started to run again, upsetting a couple of crows who had found something in the expanse to peck. They cawed at him and circled, bobbing through the air as though they would plummet to the ground if they stopped flapping, incapable of gliding. Field stopped running. He had dozens miles to cover and nobody would bother following him into the countryside. They would be waiting in town.

He wasn't sure how to get there. The highway was out of sight. The sun was a faint idea behind the slab of slate-colored clouds, but enough of its light was visible descending on the western horizon, so he knew which direction to walk. The next batch of hills had a higher concentration of oak trees sprouting from them, so he was getting closer. He wouldn't be able to make it before nightfall, though, and he needed to figure out where he would go when he made it home, because he couldn't really go home. He found a soft spot under one of the oak trees on the top of a hill, the dirt slackened by a colony of ground squirrel tunnels. He watched as the sun revealed itself from under the clouds just before it disappeared behind the other end of the earth. He said a prayer for Yadi, and considered where he might find sanctuary.

I had taken maybe three steps from my car in the staff parking lot when he whispered to me from behind.

He was covered in dirt and dead grass.

"I'm sorry," he said. "I don't know where else to go."

I told him there was no need to apologize, that I'd be glad to help.

"You don't have to do very much," he assured me. "I just need a safe place where I can make some things happen."

I let him in the car and went to the office to tell them I might not be in the rest of the day. When I returned and saw him slouched down below the level of the window, I confess I started to get nervous. And that was before he told me the latest developments and showed me the gun.

We stared at it as the washing machine rattled through the spin cycle in the background. He had laid it on our dining room table when he handed me his clothes to be washed, dressed in a pair of my husband's sweatpants that barely reached past his shins, and a sweatshirt that looked like he had rolled up the sleeves even though he had not.

"I wish I could use it on Gonzo," he said.

"That wouldn't solve anything."

"I know. But it would feel good."

"To kill someone?"

He looked away from the gun but kept his eyes down on the table top.

"I only said 'I wish,'" he reminded me.

"You're handling this the way it needs to be handled. The least dramatic way is going to get the most dramatic results."

"You still repeat words a lot when you talk to me."

"I probably do that with everyone by now, even off the job. I've been working at it for so long."

He continued to address the table rather than me, but would shift his focus to different parts of it.

"I waited too long to handle it," he said. "It should never have come this far."

"I could have done more, too," I laid my hand across the table, hoping he would take it.

"That's not true," he ignored my offer. "I wasn't a kid anymore."

I slid my hand away and let it fall into my lap.

"Yet here we are," I said.

I joined him in looking at the table with the gun on it.

The washing machine stopped and I went to switch his clothes to the dryer. I held up his wrestling hoodie by the shoulders and contemplated the school logo before adding it to the pile, shutting the door, and pressing the button.

"I didn't see the agent's card in any of your pockets," I said when I sat back down with him.

"I know the number. I stared at it a lot over the holidays."

"When do you want to make the call?"

"There's something I'd like to do first."

"Okay."

"Two things, actually."

"Okay..."

He spoke to my hesitation.

By the time the bell sounded on the dryer, he had explained his plan and provided me with enough of a reason for each move to convince me.

The first stop was a last visit to Lulu.

He wasn't sure it would lead anywhere, but he had to try. We packed the gun in the trunk to hand over later and headed east.

We pulled over about a mile before reaching The Crossroads. When no cars were visible in either direction, Field jumped out and scrambled down to the canal. He would follow it to the back of the shopping center, and I would tell Lulu where to find him. I drove onward, parked a couple of storefronts away from the gift shop per his instructions, and gave him some time to reach his destination. Out of curiosity I looked around to see if anyone appeared to be keeping Lulu under surveillance, as Field so strongly suspected. There were a couple of candidates. A lone man in a sleek sedan could have been there on behalf of the crime family. A van could have been filled with federal agents. Observing each for a few minutes didn't offer much of a chance to draw any conclusions, only leap to them.

Lulu wanted to hug me when she recognized me, and I wanted to hug her, but I stuck to the plan and verbally kept her at arm's length.

"Someone may be watching me?" she processed my excuse for keeping my distance.

"Only to try and catch Field if they see him."

She stood up straight into a sigh.

"He's in back," I confirmed what she seemed to suspect. "Maybe down by the canal. Maybe right by the door. I don't know. He's somewhere back there."

Her first reaction was to shake her head.

"He's turning himself in," I explained. "It's your last chance to see him."

"I'll visit him in prison someday. Maybe."

"He may not go to prison since he's helping the investigators. He'll probably have to disappear."

She started to seem capable of relenting.

"It would mean the world to him," I pressed.

She spent some time in her mind, then nodded and walked to the back exit.

He was on the walkway right outside the door, which startled her.

"Thank you for coming," he said.

She shrugged.

"I was going to write a letter, but that's never gone very well for me."

She alternated between looking out at the countryside and at Field.

"Did Madeline tell you I'm turning myself in?"

She nodded.

"Are going to say anything?"

"Do you want a medal?" she snapped.

"No. I want to say goodbye."

"Well..."

She couldn't get the next word out.

"Goodbye?" Field offered to complete her sentence.

"You're the only person who makes me cry."

Field moved toward her, but she held up her hand while she braced herself against any tears that threatened to fall.

He obeyed her command.

"You're the only person who gets me to do the right thing," he told her while respecting her space.

He hoped she would give in and open her arms.

"I should go," he said when it was clear that would not happen.

She nodded and continued to compose herself.

He hesitated. He wanted to try and hug her one more time, but couldn't bear the thought of being denied again. He turned and was about to head down the hill.

"Would you have done the right thing if you didn't find out who she was?" she asked.

He stopped.

"Would you have turned yourself in if I wasn't related to her?" she rephrased the question.

He understood. He had been asking himself the same thing for some time. The answer had always been the same, and he was hoping for a different one for her sake. He looked across the valley and took a deep breath, trying to clear his mind for a new answer to arrive, but none came. He was stuck with the same one.

He looked at her.

"I don't know," he said.

She may have appreciated his honesty, she may have been shocked by it. He couldn't tell. She looked as though she was listening to a longer explanation that only she could hear. She took a quick glance of her own at the valley, then went back inside.

Field walked back down to the canal.

Tumbleweeds of all shapes and sizes were pinned along the chain link fence that spanned the shoreline. New ones would roll into the line as he retraced his path, blown by the wind from wherever their journey started.

When he climbed into the car, he asked me if I knew what kind of plants tumbleweeds came from. All I could remember is that they were from another part of the world, brought over by someone who thought they could build a business on them. But their roots couldn't take hold. They would grow larger than their base could handle, break away, and tumble across the countryside until they hit a fence, a wall, or a corner.

"I wonder whose idea it was," Field speculated.

"I have a feeling we don't know, because I'm sure they washed their hands of it as their failure propagated."

I braced myself for another tumbleweed question, maybe what 'propagated' means, as he clearly didn't want to talk about his conversation with Lulu. When he chose to avoid the topic with silence instead, I considered expanding on the history of tumbleweeds, maybe using it as a symbol of Gonzo's business as a prelude to asking what happened behind the gift shop. But given Field's frame of mind, he wouldn't hear most of it. So after a few miles, I simply cracked.

"Two of my favorite people said goodbye to each other and I'm supposed to just drive?"

"You can ask her what happened," he said. "Next time you see her." He smiled.

I was happy to see him do so, but reminded him there were limits on how far I could see his plan through.

"All I can do is encourage her to apply and to use me as a reference," I said. "I won't even be on the hiring committee. It'll be the teachers and the other tutors. And the principal. Of course."

"Lulu's the perfect fit. And she'll nail the interview."

He focused on the road ahead.

He was right about Lulu, but that wasn't the reason he signaled that his assessment was the last word.

We still had one more stop to make.

We parked neither in the front nor the back of the home store. We stopped on the side, where the contractors pick up their lumber.

He passed through a cavernous door that could have been the entrance to a castle with a drawbridge leading to it. An employee spotted him.

"I like that hoodie!" he hollered. "Haven't seen that in a while!"

Field waved at him without breaking stride.

He marched to Gonzo's office.

Gonzo was slumped in his chair, looking out the window but slouched too low to see the showroom floor, only the ceiling and its crosses of steel beams.

When he saw Field, he spun the chair slowly to face him, as though he hadn't moved in hours.

"Right now," Field snarled.

"What?"

"Me and you," Field crouched slightly and beckoned him over.

"You're kidding," Gonzo smirked.

"Just once!" Field roared. "Let's keep it simple for once!"

Gonzo took a deep breath.

"This is how you imagined the ending?"

"No, I imagine you in jail. But first I want to kick your ass."

Gonzo nearly smiled, but dismissed it with a puff of air.

"Yadi won his fight with that guy from the family," he said. "And it didn't matter."

Field stood up straight and lowered his defenses.

"Enrique?"

"Is that his name?"

"What happened to Yadi?"

"I don't know anything anymore," Gonzo shrugged.

"Another lie."

"When have I lied to you before, Field?"

"You lied about the business."

"I withheld information."

"Oh come on," Field scoffed. "Talk, talk, talk."

"I revealed the truth a little bit at a time."

"You lied about why you wanted me to wrestle."

"I wasn't grooming you for the business, if that's what you're getting at. I wanted you on the team because I knew you were going to be great."

"That's what you say."

"It's true."

"You can't prove it."

"Yes I can. Ask anyone who saw your talent, who saw your potential. They'll tell you. And the best part is you lived up to everyone's expectations. The world is full of people who didn't live up to their potential. You did."

Field didn't want to hear that.

"What happened to Yadi?" he demanded.

Gonzo exhaled, and his life expectancy appeared to decline by a decade by the time he breathed in.

"I don't know the details," he confessed. "But it's not good."

"Is he gone?"

Gonzo nodded.

Field didn't know what to do with himself.

"You want to sit down?" Gonzo gestured to one of the chairs in front of his desk.

Field took him up on his offer.

"It didn't used to be like this," Gonzo lamented. "It was a lot more straightforward. Simple. We used to be paid up front. No debts. That's when the problems started. We became a goddamn credit bureau, a bank. But the borders kept tightening up so nobody dared go back once they made it across. It wasn't enough just to get them work. The costs started to soar. I thought the merger with the family would help."

"It was still illegal," Field reminded him.

Gonzo chuckled sadly.

"Yes, it was."

"So why did you do it?"

"Ah," Gonzo leaned back in his chair. "You want answers. Was that the play all along? You knew I wouldn't take you up on your ridiculous wrestling match. Or did you honestly think I'd wrestle you, and now you're on to Plan B?"

"I just want to know."

"Well I'm not that kind of mentor, son. People come to me because I get things done. Those are the kinds of answers I provide. There was a demand, and I knew how to fill it. I'm all about how, not why."

"That doesn't seem like a very smart way to live."

"Smart?" Gonzo rose from his chair. "You're gonna lecture me on being smart?"

"Maybe that's not the right word."

Gonzo came around the desk.

"You picked one hell of a time in life to start reinventing yourself."

"I've just been thinking."

He crouched in front of Field.

"Is that really a good idea?"

"Wanting to know why we do things doesn't seem like such a bad idea."

Gonzo clutched each side of the chair in which Field sat.

"Questions are frustrating," he said. "They never end. One leads to another, and another, and another. I tell you why I started my business, to meet a demand, but then you wonder why that demand exists in the first place, and if meeting that demand is moral, and who decides what's moral, and on and on and on and on..."

Gonzo stood up.

"You know what?" he said. "Fuck it. Let's wrestle. You were right the first time."

He backed up and hunched over, giving Field some space and gesturing at him to fill it.

Field stood up and kicked the chairs out of the way.

They sized each other up in a slow-moving circle.

"Make your move, dumb ass," Gonzo taunted him.

Field wanted to say something back, but was too busy trying to stay calm and not take the bait.

"I know, I know," Gonzo kept it up. "You may be dumb, but you've got heart. You've got morals. Or maybe that's just what they say about dumb people to make them feel better."

Field launched himself into Gonzo's midsection.

Gonzo rode Field's momentum and used it against him, rolling him over and pinning him with minimal effort. He locked onto Field's right arm and forced it upwards along his back.

"Do you feel that?" Gonzo gasped.

Field grunted in pain.

"I can dislocate your shoulder. Pop. Just like that. Then there's this other move I can make while I've got you down here, I can break your arm. I can break your leg, I can choke you. Really choke you. To death. All these moves I couldn't teach you because they were against the rules."

He released him and stayed on the floor, leaning back against the wall under the window.

Field turned over and sat on his knees.

They took some time to catch their breath.

When their panting died down, Gonzo looked at Field and waited to speak until Field looked back.

"I had a decision to make years ago," he said. "I made a bad one. And it's led to a hundred more. Some worse than others."

He stared past Field, perhaps recalling those decisions. Field imagined he was really only thinking of Yadi.

"Here you are in the same position," he regained his focus on Field. "I'm jealous."

He turned away.

"Now go do it."

Field used my phone.

He said the walk to my car was the longest he had ever taken in his life. He kept looking over his shoulder as he made his way across the home store floor, wondering if Gonzo would change his mind and chase him down. Every time one of his co-workers would yell "Field!", he thought it was to warn him that Gonzo or Enrique or someone he had never seen before was behind him, but all they were doing was waving.

They were waving hello.

Field waved back, but he was saying goodbye.

The trial was closed to the public due to the involvement of organized crime. The prosecution's star witness would not have testified in open court, anyway. We were never going to be treated to a moment when Field would be asked if the man who ordered the hit on Sylvia Carbajal was in the courtroom, and Field would say 'yes' and point at Gonzo, and the attorney would say 'let the record show that Mr. Spahn has identified Coach Helio Gonzalez.' We were not going to hear Field tell the tale of Yadi's sacrifice, listening like children at story time. We had no chance to weep together as the attorney would hold up the gun Field escaped with and proclaim it was traced back to the crew who tracked down Yadi outside his home later that same day as he was packing his truck to drive north, to go in a new direction. There were no speeches made in anger by Dante or Lulu. No public apologies from Field or Gonzo. The members of the crime family who were indicted were not paraded out from the shadows and into court, nor were any law enforcement officers who were found complicit. They were all just names in the articles that everyone in town read closely and discussed.

The discussions were not always cordial. Whatever passions were unable to be expressed in court played out in diners during breakfast and lunch rushes, in grocery aisles, check-out lines, and on the floor of the home store. Everyone read the same reports, but took from them what they brought to them. One of the most contentious debates involved Field's place in the Ring of Honor. Some thought his name should stay, since he broke up the crime ring. Others thought his name should be taken down. But that's all he was, a name, from the moment he made the call.

Agent Barajas asked for his location, told him to stay where he was, and arrived with local law enforcement in a matter of minutes. We never said goodbye. We exchanged bewildered stares, both of us overwhelmed by the speed at which everything was happening. All that he did to help the investigation was conducted behind closed doors. With no family, it was easy to make him disappear. He probably could have done it on his own, without their help.

For I imagine they weren't aware he came back to pay a visit.

None of us actually saw him. I found an envelope on my windshield early in the new school year after Gonzo and his managing partners had finally been sentenced. It was a standard letter-sized envelope, but heavier than I expected, as there was more than a letter inside.

A flat piece of rusted metal was wrapped inside a note that read, "Please bury this in the field where Lulu first brought out the best in me. She'll know where that is."

The metal plate had a handmade inscription engraved on it:

*Field + Lulu > Field - Lulu*

I showed it to her during lunch as she watched her charges in the Special Ed Program swarm the playground. Her first instinct was to look around to see if she could spot him somewhere on the fringe.

"That field is hard as a rock," I said. "We might want to wait until we get some rain."

"The sprinkler still leaks," she smiled. "I'll grab some shovels from the garden project and see you there after school."

"You don't want to get the kids involved?"

"God, no," she rolled her eyes. "They'll dig it up within a day to show the other kids, then start digging holes of their own and burying our classroom supplies until there's none left. And no grass on the field. Nothing but little piles of dirt."

I laughed and agreed to meet her after the students had been excused.

She did share the metal plate with them.

I arrived at their room before the final bell rang. Her group table was closest to the door, so I was able to observe the lesson inconspicuously. One of the students had the potential to be the next Lulu, while the other three were boys who likely faced challenging futures due to their remoteness from the world at large, embodied by some form of either restlessness or stillness.

"Does anyone remember what this symbol means?" she pointed at the 'greater than' sign.

One of the boys who tended to stare out the window quite a bit sprung to life.

"It means there's a greedy alligator!"

Lulu chuckled, since she was looking for the definition rather than the reminder.

"That's right," she went with it. "And what does that greedy alligator want?"

"More!" they all said.

"He wants what's greater, right?"

"Yes!" most of them said.

"But look at this," she pointed at the names. "These aren't numbers."

"They're names!" the boy stayed involved.

"Your name!" said the young Lulu.

"One of them is my name, yes."

"You have a funny name," said a boy who often said things were funny.

"I do," she laughed. "I do have a funny name. You've told me that before many times. And this name over here, this other name, that's the name of my friend who was in this program with me."

"His name is Field?" said young Lulu.

"It is," Lulu didn't want to focus on his name, but who he was. "I've told you about me being right where you are now. But I haven't told you about my friend. We were the best of friends, and we always wanted to be something great, just like any kid wants to be. But not many people thought we could be. And sometimes we weren't so sure, either. We doubted ourselves. But we helped each other, and he ended up doing something really great after all."

"What did he do?" asked the boy who no doubt hoped it was something funny.

"It's a long story," Lulu apologized. "Some other time. I promise."

"And you did something great," said young Lulu.

"I did?"

"You became our teacher."

"Tutor," Lulu corrected her and grinned at me. "We don't want to upset Ms. Gretchen. She's your teacher."

The boy who hadn't contributed yet, who rarely ever did, still stared at the metal plate.

"But this says he's better with you than without you," he concluded his study of it. "Just him. It's not about both of you."

Lulu and I exchanged impressed looks while the other students agreed with him.

"Did your friend make that?" asked young Lulu.

"Yes, he did."

"Do you feel the same way?" she followed up.

Lulu considered the question.

"Yes," she decided. "I do. If I made one of these, I would switch around the order of the names."

"You should do that!" the suddenly gregarious boy said.

"Yeah!" came various versions of "You should do that and give it to him!"

Lulu smiled at them, and at me, and as we dug a hole later in the bog surrounding the sprinkler head that was still leaking after twenty years, she smiled at no one in particular.

"We should shake it," she said, holding up the metal square.

"He probably already did that," I laughed.

"Just in case."

We each took a turn flapping the sheet of metal before placing it in the hole.

When we finished topping off the dirt, she leaned on her shovel and surveyed the area.

"Looking for someone?" I asked.

"No," she continued her contemplation. "Just letting some memories flow."

"What do you see?"

"It's more of a feeling."

I left it at that.

It was hers.

I had a similar feeling years later, in that I kept it to myself.

We were at Disneyland with our grandchildren, fending off their latest request to raid one the gift shops on Main Street. The kind of minor clamor that happens whenever a character emerges to pose and shake hands with the masses started to build.

I thought it was Donald Duck in an old-fashioned pilot outfit, but the kids corrected me.

"That's not Donald," my grandson drawled as though I could not have said anything more stupid. "It's Launchpad McQuack."

"Oh," I said, the name not resonating. "I guess he is a little tall to be Donald."

"He's Scrooge McDuck's pilot," my granddaughter filled in my blankness.

"Ah, I know that name."

"But I don't remember any airplanes in *A Christmas Carol*," my husband chimed in.

"It's a newer version of Scrooge," my grandson hopped back on his high horse. "He's not a Christmas character anymore. He has his own series."

My granddaughter ran some gentle interference again, explaining how Launchpad doesn't just fly Scrooge around, he protects the Duck family. People think he's big and dumb, because he screws up a lot, but he ends up doing the right thing.

At least that's the gist of what she said. I can't remember the details, because toward the end of her description, the person in the Launchpad McQuack costume took a keen interest in me. My granddaughter was initially too intent on finishing his biography to notice, but my grandson did, and he suddenly thought I was brilliant.

Launchpad shook with exaggerated reverence when he saw me, leaning back and wiggling his hands in the air, pointing at me in between bursts of mock euphoria to confirm I was the subject of his reaction. He approached and bowed at the waist repeatedly before me, both arms extended in a gesture of supplication and unworthiness. That's when my granddaughter caught on.

"Does he think you're somebody famous?" she asked.

"Or powerful?" my husband teased.

Our grandson was too busy laughing to contribute any guesses.

When the person inside the suit put his index finger up to where his lips would be if ducks had lips, I had a guess of my own.

I almost said his name out loud, but the duck tapped his finger to his beak more emphatically when he saw the glow of recognition on my face.

Maybe it was a case of mistaken identity, as my family suspected. Maybe I reminded whomever was in the costume of somebody else, especially since it must be hard to see through the mesh portholes that allow them to not be completely dependent on their spotter. But I stuck with my guess that I didn't tell anyone.

Not even Lulu.

"Why Launchpad?" she asked the first time she saw the framed photograph on my desk. "Didn't you get any pictures with Mickey or Donald?"

"Sure," I said, looking at the smiling duck costume, imagining the person inside smiling along with the rest of us in the photo. "But I like the way we look in this one."

"It's always about us, isn't it?" Lulu half-joked.

"Always," I fully agreed.

# Also by Sean Boling

**The Current Mr. Orr**
Devin's Best Afterlife
Once in Two Lifetimes
Revenge and Wellness in the Sweet Hereafter


**Standalone**
Cut Flowers
Abraham the Anchor Baby Terrorist
Pigs and Other Living Things
The Summer of Our Foreclosure
Satellite Campus
A Charter to That Other Place
The Latest Version of My Love Story
Show Them What They Won
The Name Field
Should
Moral Adjacent
Over Here We Have

# About the Author

Sean lives with his family in Templeton, California. He teaches English at Cuesta College.